'Can't you just leave things alone?'

'By "things", I take it you mean you?' Blade smiled coldly. 'You are still my wife, Amy!'

'You don't scare me,' Amy lied bravely. 'And I don't like threats.'

'Then take it as a warning—one you can pass on to interested parties—you are my property as far as I see it, and *no one* steals what is mine!'

Dear Reader

Here we are once again at the end of the year... looking forward to Christmas and to the delightful surprises the new year holds. During the festivities, though, make sure you let Mills & Boon help you to enjoy a few precious hours of escape. For, with our latest selection of books, you can meet the men of your dreams and travel to far-away places—without leaving the comfort of your own fireside!

Till next month,

The Editor

Helen Brooks lives in Northamptonshire and is married with three children. As she is a committed Christian, busy housewife and mother, her spare time is at a premium but her hobbies include reading, swimming, gardening and walking her two energetic, inquisitive and very endearing young dogs. Her long-cherished aspiration to write became a reality when she put pen to paper on reaching the age of forty, and sent the result off to Mills & Boon.

Recent titles by the same author:

BITTER HONEY
KNIGHT IN BLACK VELVET
THE SULTAN'S FAVOURITE
WEB OF DARKNESS

LOVERS
NOT FRIENDS

BY

HELEN BROOKS

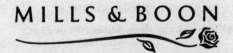

MILLS & BOON LIMITED
ETON HOUSE, 18-24 PARADISE ROAD
RICHMOND, SURREY TW9 1SR

All the characters in this book have no existence outside the imagination of the Author, and have no relation whatsoever to anyone bearing the same name or names. They are not even distantly inspired by any individual known or unknown to the Author, and all the incidents are pure invention.

MILLS & BOON and the Rose Device
are trademarks of the publisher.

First published in Great Britain 1994
by Mills & Boon Limited

© Helen Brooks 1994

Australian copyright 1994   Philippine copyright 1994
This edition 1994

ISBN 0 263 78765 6

Set in Times Roman 10½ on 12 pt.
01-9412-52023 C

Made and printed in Great Britain

CHAPTER ONE

'YOU know I'll never let you go, don't you? I'd rather kill you than let anyone else have you.'

'Blade——'

'Don't Blade me! You're mine, Amy, you'll always be mine—one way or another.'

'You're crazy——'

'About you? Maybe——' the glittering black eyes were merciless '—but you know me well enough by now to know that I'm not in the habit of making idle threats. You'll pay for what you've done. Believe me, I can make you wish you'd never been born. And when the payment is over——' the hard handsome face could have been carved in stone '—you'll still be my wife, *my wife*, Amy.'

'No!' The tortured scream that was wrenched from her throat brought her awake in one violent movement as she jerked upright in the small narrow bed. It was a dream, just a dream . . . She brought her knees up to her chest, wrapping her arms round her legs as she let her pounding heart slow into a more normal rhythm. He wasn't here, he hadn't found her . . . *yet*. The dream was still too vivid to let her keep back the fears she held at bay in the clear light of day. He *would* find her. She shook her head with a little moan as the silky sweep of soft golden hair covered her damp face. She had been mad to run away like that; she should have thought it out properly, made plans. No one

crossed Blade Forbes and got away with it, no one,
let alone his young wife of six months. His power and
influence stretched long tentacles everywhere; what
could she *do*?

Nothing. She climbed out of the bed wearily,
padding across the small square room and flicking
the switch on the coffee-maker with a long sigh as she
glanced out of the high, narrow window, her gaze
moving past the old stone wall holding the overgrown
garden in check, and out over the green fields rising
steeply into the distance. The cold grey light of early
morning was filling the small room with a dull glow,
but outside the harsh sweep of sky was swept clean
in readiness for a new day.

Blade. She wrapped her arms tightly round her waist
as she let herself think, really think for the first time
in weeks. Blade Forbes, American business tycoon
extraordinaire, hard, dynamic, with a reputation for
ruthlessness that bordered on the extreme, and yet . . .
She shut her eyes tightly as her thoughts sped on. With
her he had been gentle, tender, loving, displaying an
understanding that she had never dreamed possible
in such an arrogant, masculine man. She swayed
slightly as the agony that filled every waking moment
with a dull ache swamped her afresh, racking her
slender body with physical pain. They had been so
happy, so in love.

'Stop it, Amy.' She spoke out loud into the empty
room, her beautiful delicate face white with strain.
These endless post-mortems would do no good; it was
over, irrevocably over. Loving him as she did, she had
had no choice but to leave, and nothing had changed.

As she got ready for work later that morning, the dull, damp start to the day had changed with the mercurial capriciousness of English weather into bright sunshine, a fragrant wave of fresh Yorkshire air filling the small room with the scents of thick moorland turf and wild flowers from the hills beyond, reminding her that summer was just around the corner. This would have been her first summer as a married woman...

The thought was still with her as she arrived at the small restaurant just after one but, within minutes, the hectic bustle in the tiny kitchen had reduced the gnawing pain to the familiar background ache.

She had been lucky to find this job, she thought quietly, glancing round the shining room that was filled to capacity if more than a few people had the misfortune to be in it at the same time. When she had arrived in the Yorkshire Dales three months ago, stunned and shattered at the enormous step she had taken, she hadn't had any definite thought for the future beyond hiding for a few weeks out of Blade's reach before maybe trying to make her way abroad.

But then the calm, slow peace of the place had worked its spell on her sore heart, and when her money had run out she had heard about this job from the motherly landlady of the tiny guest-house where she was staying. She didn't want to use a penny of the vast bank account Blade had set up for her; that part of her life was over with for good, and so it was essential she provide for herself.

The previous assistant cook, waitress and jack-of-all-trades had up and left with a visiting salesman, leaving her husband and children in the process. 'A flighty piece if ever I did see one,' Mrs Cox had gri-

maced disapprovingly, nodding her grey head like a
plump, well-fed little pigeon, and the owner of the
restaurant had welcomed Amy with open arms even
before he had heard about the three-year course she
had completed at college in catering economics.

And so she had stayed. As she ladled thick meaty
home-made soup into squat earthenware bowls, she
reflected on the intricacy of the web of life. It had
been her job that had first brought her into Blade's
life and now it was the means of allowing her to
survive away from him. She needed the long hours
and hard work more than her employer would ever
know.

'All right, Amy?' She came out of her reverie to
find Arthur Kelly watching her mildly, his blunt
Yorkshireman's face enquiring. 'Feeling under the
weather, lass?'

'No, I'm fine, Arthur. I'm sorry, I was just daydreaming.' She smiled quickly as she placed the bowls
on the tray and prepared to leave the kitchen for the
dining area beyond. Arthur was typical of the average
Yorkshire native, kind, forthright, but holding to the
principle of minding his own business, for which she
was supremely grateful. Both her landlady and employer must have wondered at her abrupt arrival into
their little community, but they had asked no questions, either directly or indirectly, even when at times
the deep mauve shadows under her eyes must have
spoken volumes.

She had just placed the two bowls of steaming soup,
along with a basket of freshly baked bread rolls, in
front of the young couple who had ordered them when
the old traditional bell on the front door jangled a

new arrival. She felt no presentiment as she turned, no apprehension or sixth sense to warn her that her fragile equilibrium was about to be blown apart.

'Hello, Amy.' His voice was quiet, too quiet, and the narrowed eyes were deadly.

'Blade...' As her face drained of colour she was conscious, for one piercing moment, of a rush of fierce joy at seeing him again, which was quite ridiculous in the circumstances, and then, as the full horror of the situation swept in on her, she thought for one desperate moment that she was going to faint.

He obviously had the same notion because he moved quickly, forcing her roughly down on to a seat, his voice harsh. 'Don't look so surprised. You knew I would find you one day; it was just a matter of time.'

'Blade...' She found she was incapable of saying anything but his name; her mind seemed to have frozen into an icy void with no coherent thought that she was conscious of.

'The very same.' The glittering black eyes held her dazed blue ones ruthlessly, his arrogant, handsome face as hard as stone, just as in the dream. The dream... She caught at the thought faintly. It had been a warning; she had somehow sensed he was near. She should have been on her guard, should have *known*... 'Now get up.'

'What?' She stared at him numbly.

'I said get up.' The look on his face would have terrified her if she hadn't been beyond feeling anything, but now she heard the young couple stir behind her and then the man appeared at their side.

'I say, look here.' He couldn't have been more than twenty-one and was clearly scared to death. 'Is everything all right, miss?' He was speaking directly to her; his eyes had flicked once to Blade's dark countenance which had turned his frightened face still whiter. 'Shall I call someone?'

'No——'

Her voice was lost as Blade's low growl cut into the thick, tense air. 'Don't interfere in things that don't concern you, sonny.' He didn't look at the youth as he spoke; his eyes hadn't moved from her face since he had entered the restaurant.

'Look, I don't think she wants to speak to you——'

Blade cut off the young man's voice by the simple expedient of turning the full force of that malignant gaze on to the blanched face, and even in her frozen state Amy felt a dart of admiration for the boy because he didn't turn tail and run. 'Go and sit down in your seat.' His accent was very pronounced, which somehow made the softly snarled words even more chilling. 'Or I will personally place you there.'

'Stop this.' As Army rose jerkily to her feet, she caught the glimpse of terror in the young man's face and suddenly hot anger replaced the frozen calm. 'Don't bully him.'

'Bully him?' Blade's big body stiffened, and she felt a moment of churning fear before she turned quickly to the youth.

'It's all right, really. Please go and have your meal.'

'Are you sure?' Relief was warring with male pride, but relief won as he scuttled off back to his waiting girlfriend who had been viewing the proceedings with avid interest.

'What do you want, Blade?' She had to tilt her head back to look into his face. At over six feet he had always dwarfed her five-foot, four-inch petiteness, but in the flat canvas shoes she wore for a working day he seemed even larger.

'You know exactly what I want, so don't try and play dumb.' The dark fury that had transfigured his face was new to her; she had never seen him angry before. Coolly cutting when someone had annoyed him, cynically mocking with a sardonic deadly bite on more than one occasion, but he had always been perfectly in control as though it were all a game. But this was no game. The black eyes blazed back at her as she met them square on. And no one knew that better than she. 'Are you coming out of here with me of your own accord or do I have to carry you out?'

'I can't just leave, I work here——'

'Oh, you can, Amy.' The intonation his accent gave her name still had the power to make her weak at the knees, she reflected dazedly. 'And that is exactly what you are going to do.'

'I'm not coming back, Blade——'

'Who asked you to?' There was a hard grimness in his face that had never been there before when he looked at her. 'You don't really think I would want you back after what you've done, do you? That I still care? That would make me the biggest fool alive.' Something flickered in the back of his eyes as he spoke, swiftly veiled, and his voice was even harsher as he continued, 'But I do want to talk to you and I want to know where he is. You understand me? You are both going to learn a lesson you'll never forget.'

'Where he is?' She repeated his words vaguely with the helpless realisation that she had lost her grasp on the situation. 'Who?'

'I told you, don't mess with me, Amy.' His grip on her arm was vice-like and again she heard the couple behind them stir. 'I've stood all I'm going to take.'

She would have to talk with him. As she stared back into his dark face, it was stamped with the ruthless determination that had brought him from the relative obscurity of second son of a mining engineer in his native America to self-made millionaire at the age of thirty-five when she had first met him a year ago. His toughness was legendary, his inflexibility when he wanted something rock-like. Yes, she would have to talk with him, and the sooner she got it over and done with, the better.

'I'll just ask Arthur if I can leave for a while—my boss, he's out there...' She waved vaguely towards the kitchen door.

'You do that.' His grip lessened and she was free. 'I'll give you exactly sixty seconds.'

Fifty-nine seconds later, as she emerged with Blade from the warm interior of the restaurant into the ancient winding village street, she took a deep steadying breath of the pure Yorkshire air before following him to his car.

'Can't we just walk?' she asked nervously, as they reached the low-slung sports car that was crouched broodingly in the grey street. 'I'd rather——'

'I'm not interested in what you'd rather,' Blade said coldly as he opened the passenger door and indicated that she slide in. 'You'll do as you're told.'

He had never used that tone of voice with her before, and suddenly everything in her rebelled against the arrogant authority that had been paramount since she had set eyes on him again.

'You can't order me about like this, Blade.' She tried to keep her voice firm and cool, but she was unable to hide the quiver of pain in its depths. 'I'm filing for divorce, as you know; you have no right——'

'Damn my rights!' His voice was vitriolic with pure rage. 'I've never let "my rights" as you call them interfere with what I want before. Fortunately in this case that is not a problem. I don't want you, Amy, if that makes you feel a little more comfortable. The only feeling you inspire in me is one of disgust and contempt. Got it?'

She'd brought this on herself and she couldn't blame him, she really couldn't, but the torturous pain that was constricting her chest was making it difficult to breathe. She had intended that he forget her, maybe even hate her if that made it easier, but that had been before she saw him again. She couldn't bear this, she really couldn't . . . 'Then why——' Her voice cracked and she swallowed before trying again. 'Why did you find me?'

'Because, like it or not, you are still my wife for the moment and I'm damned if I'll allow you to walk out on me without an explanation. There is also the little matter of retribution.' The black eyes were as hard as granite. 'So just get in the car, Amy, and keep that beautiful, deceitful mouth closed if you know what is good for you.' His voice was smooth and controlled and infinitely dangerous.

Once in the car he drove swiftly through the village, past the cobbled market place with its market cross and thirteenth-century church, and up the steep one-in-four hill on the other side that the powerful car took completely in its stride. He didn't speak again, concentrating on the narrow twisting road contained within old stone walls that were as ancient as time. After long taut minutes she risked a glance under her eyelashes at the harsh, handsome profile, her stomach tightening as she took in the clear tanned skin, straight nose and heavy shock of burnished brown hair. His face had been etched in her mind with painful clarity for the first few days after she had left, but it had been three months now and the image had begun to fade. She loved him, how she loved him, she would never stop loving him——

'Right, now we'll have it all.' He swung the car off the road into a small gateway that looked across a huge backcloth of walled green fields, scattered farmhouses and rolling undulating hills that seemed to stretch into infinity. 'And I do mean *all*, Amy, and a word of caution.' He turned in his seat and took her chin in his hand, drawing her face round so that her eyes met the stony hardness of his. 'If you lie to me and I find out, I'll make you regret the day you were born. I want the truth, however unpalatable. Do you understand?'

Yes, she understood all right, she thought miserably as her heart pounded with fear. But the truth was the one thing she could never give him. She couldn't bear to see the knowledge dawn on that loved face of what the future would hold, the pity, the despair he would feel for her, the desperation to put things right that were for once totally out of his control. And then the waiting for the monstrous thing to happen. No. She had been right to leave and now, somehow, she had to cement the break into place. But how could she begin? How could she look him in the face and tell him she didn't love him, without him guessing it was a lie?

'If it helps you start, I know about John Davies.' The cold voice at her side was now quite expressionless, and he turned to stare out of the windscreen into the world beyond lit with sunshine. 'The private detective I hired to find you also found out about your "friend". Unfortunately he wasn't there when I called,' he finished grimly.

'You went to John's house?' she asked faintly. 'But why——'

'Don't give me that, Amy!' He turned with such savagery that her stomach lurched into her mouth. 'How long have you known him? When did it start?'

'Start?' She heard him literally grind his teeth in his rage, and forced her mind into gear. He thought she had left him for John? Sweet, uncomplicated John who had been her friend for years?

'I remember his name from the wedding invitation list.' Blade's voice was as hard as stone. 'But he didn't come. Now I understand why.'

'He didn't come because he's been in Spain for the last three years,' she said tightly. 'He's——'

'Dead when I get hold of him,' Blade finished grimly.

'John has nothing to do with this.' She found she was wringing her hands in her anguish and forced them into tight fists in her lap. 'He sent me a postcard

a few months ago with his new address to say he was
back in England, and when I left it was the only place
I could think of to go. I didn't even stay a night with
him. He put me in touch with a lady in the village
who takes in the occasional guest——'

'Mrs Cox,' Blade stated stonily. 'Yes, I know. I also
know that you see him on a pretty regular basis, so
do us both a favour and cut the bull, Amy.'

She stared at him helplessly as her mind flew on.
Maybe she should let him think she *had* left him for
John? She felt his impatient movement at her side,
and turned quickly to speak. The note she had left
had stated only that she considered their marriage had
been a terrible mistake and that she had decided, une-
quivocally, that it was over. That she wanted no
settlement, nothing from him, and that divorce proceedings would start immediately. He was a fiercely
proud, implacable man. If he thought she had left
him for a lover, that knock to his male ego would be
unspeakable and final. And this had to be final.

'My relationship with John is nothing to do with
you,' she said quietly. 'I don't——'

'The hell it isn't!' he ground out through closed
teeth as he studied her set face with harsh black eyes.
'You took me for one hell of a ride, sweetheart, and
no one, *no one*, does that. When I get hold of him...'
His voice stopped but the look on his dark face was
lethal.

'This is ridiculous,' she said, with as much calm as
she could muster through the racing fury of her
heartbeat. 'Hurting John won't do any good, I'll never
come back——'

'You'll never get the chance,' he interrupted brutally. 'You're soiled merchandise and I only have the best.' She knew he was lashing out through his own hurt, but hearing him speak like this was agonising. After all they'd shared, all the dreams for the future... 'By the time I've finished with him no other woman will want him, that much I promise you.'

'Blade——' She caught herself abruptly. What could she say now? The hole was getting deeper and deeper, but she couldn't let John take the brunt of this when all he had done was to offer comfort and refuge. 'John is a friend, nothing more.'

'Sure he is.' He opened the car door abruptly and stepped out on to the springy coarse grass beyond. 'I need some fresh air, something stinks in there.'

'I mean it, Blade.' She sprang out of the car, her voice desperate now. 'Please listen to me.'

'Listen to you?' He swung round with such ferocity that she shrank back against the comforting bulk of the car, her eyes wide with fear. 'Listen to you? Honey, you're garbage plain and simple. You think lover-boy is in for a good hiding? How right you are.' The black eyes were narrowed onyx slits. 'And there hasn't been a day in the last three months when I haven't wished you were a man so I could exact the same punishment on you personally. But——' he surveyed her with a bitter smile '—there are more ways than one to skin a rat.'

'Blade——' Her breath caught in her throat and she almost choked with fear. 'Can't you just give me a divorce and leave it at that——?'

'You'll get your divorce.' A pair of rooks suddenly swooped down over their heads from a large oak tree

at the side of the road, their harsh, raucous cry fitting
the moment perfectly, and as Blade's eyes followed
the birds she flinched at the bleakness of his profile.
But she had to do this. She had no other choice. This
might hurt now, but if she stayed with him it would
destroy him in the end. *She had no other choice*.

'Why, Amy?' As he turned to confront her, it was
the Blade she had been dreading through long restless
nights of tossing and turning and tormented dreams.
In his face was a glimpse of the Blade only she had
known, vulnerable, assailable, with a capacity for
tenderness that was unlimited. She could cope with
the fierce hostile stranger breathing fire and damn-
ation, but not this, never this. 'What went wrong?
I thought everything was so——' He stopped suddenly, turning in one harsh movement to stare out
over the hills again, his hands clenched fists in his
pockets. 'But I didn't know you, did I? It was all
make-believe, all of it.'

Oh, my darling. As she looked at the back of his
head, the sunlight turning the burnished brown gold,
she knew she was experiencing the worst that could
ever happen to her. The future, with its promise of a
living nightmare, was nothing compared to the
piercing agony that was gripping her soul in a
stranglehold, killing every spark of joy, every good
thing. She would exist from this day but she wouldn't
really be alive. But she loved him too much to take
him with her into the pit. This way he could recover
and live his life. And he *would* recover. He was a sur-
vivor. He'd forget her in time and there would be
countless women only too ready to help him.

Her eyes were dry. This pain was too deep for tears, and she turned blindly to look at a tiny farmhouse far in the distance from which a plume of smoke was slowly rising into the blue sky. 'It was just one of those things,' she said slowly as she forced the words out through stiff lips. 'Life's like that...'

'Amy?' She hadn't been aware that he had turned and was watching her, and now, as she met his eyes, she quickly schooled her features into an acceptable mask. 'There isn't something more, is there? Something you aren't telling me?'

She stared at him, her heart pounding and her mouth dry. She should have been on her guard every second, she shouldn't have relaxed for a moment. He was too intuitive, too perceptive. How many times had she seen him go straight for the jugular in the past and marvelled at his ability to see beyond the obvious, to expose every little weakness? The same attributes that made him so formidable in business were in force now and she must be careful, very careful.

'Aren't the facts enough?' she said tightly. 'Do you want more skeletons from the closet? Well, I'm sorry, I can't oblige you, Blade. You'll have to hate me for what you know; there isn't more.'

He stared at her for a whole minute, his eyes searching her face with an intentness that made her breath stop, and then he shook his head slowly, his mouth a thin white line in the starkness of his face. 'There couldn't really be more, could there?' he said with biting cynicism. 'It was just that for a minute——' He stopped abruptly and indicated the car with a violent wave of his hand. 'Get in, I've had more than enough.'

They didn't speak on the return journey, and as he drew up outside Arthur's little restaurant he leant across her and opened the door in one easy movement. 'Goodbye, Amy.' The tone was flat, all emotion gone.

'Goodbye.' She never did know how she got out of the car, but it took all the will power she possessed to walk away. She opened the door of the restaurant without looking round, hearing the car pull away with a furious roar of the powerful engine as she did so. She just made it through the kitchen door before she collapsed in a heap at Arthur Kelly's feet, her eyes big and stunned.

'Amy?' Arthur pulled her to her feet, guiding her to the one and only small stool by the back door, his lined face tight with concern. 'What on earth is it, lass? What's happened?' He patted ineffectually at her hands as he spoke, obviously quite out of his depth.

'Arthur, can I go home?' She couldn't speak for several seconds but when she did her voice was a tiny whisper. 'I feel awful.'

'You look it.' He peered distractedly through the pane of glass in the kitchen door at the customers beyond. 'I can't really take you now; I'll call a taxi, yes?'

'No, please don't.' The nearest taxi-cab service was in a small market town miles away and she needed to be alone *now*. 'I'll be home in ten minutes, I'd rather walk.'

'You don't look fit to walk, lass, let me——'

'Please, Arthur.' She faced him, her blue eyes enormous. 'I'd rather.'

'OK, lass, have it your own way.' He wrinkled his brow worriedly. 'But give me a call once you're home, eh? Just to keep an old man happy.'

'I will. And I'll see you tomorrow as usual.'

Much later that night, as Amy sat in her darkened room filled with evening shadows, after a meal cooked by the reputable Mrs Cox of which she hadn't been able to eat a bite, she forced herself to face the fact that had emerged from her meeting with Blade earlier. She had been hoping subconsciously against all reason and all logic that when she saw him again—and she had known, knowing Blade as she did, that she *would* see him again—that somehow he would work a miracle and things would be all right. It was ridiculous, insane, like a fully grown adult insisting in believing in Father Christmas when the magic had been dead for years, but a tiny part of her had clung on to the hope without her being aware of it.

In all she had had nine months with him, three of those as his wife, and it had been heaven on earth. She had been terrified that first day, as a relatively new employee of the large catering firm she worked for, when she had been called upon to liaise with the great man's secretary about a formal dinner Blade was holding that weekend. She had ventured into the massive office block with the warnings and admonitions of the other staff ringing in her ears.

'He's incredibly difficult to please, so make sure you get every little detail down on paper.'

'He never tolerates mistakes; go through things with his secretary at least twice to make sure you've got it right.'

'Don't question anything he asks for; his word is law.' The list had been endless and had reduced her to a nervous wreck before she knocked on the door to his secretary's office, which was more luxurious than her own little flat.

The room had been empty, and as she had stood in the midst of the ankle-deep carpeting, the hushed atmosphere reaching out to intimidate her still more, the catch to her case containing all the firm's literature had broken and the whole mess of papers cascaded out on to the floor. She had been on her hands and knees retrieving them with frantic haste when a deep cool male voice from the doorway froze her in her tracks.

'Miss Myatt? From Business Catering?' She raised doomed eyes to the laconic unsmiling figure leaning lazily in relaxed scrutiny as her brain had died on her. 'My secretary is indisposed today, Miss Myatt; I'm afraid you will have to talk to me.'

He was afraid? She had followed him weakly into the sumptuous office beyond the interconnecting door, setting the case down quickly, which caused it to spill open again in a repeat of the fiasco.

'Miss Myatt, this is not your day...' He moved round the desk to help, dark eyes filled with wicked amusement at her discomfiture.

Later he told her he'd fallen in love with her at that moment. 'Like a bolt of lightning,' he'd said seriously, his eyes following the smooth pure profile of her face topped by its mass of rich golden hair. She had been twenty-one and hopelessly naïve; he had been thirty-five and anything but.

He was successful, wildly handsome, with a string of much-publicised affairs credited to his account, but when he told her he had never been in love before she believed him. If it had been different he would have told her. He was that type of man. They had laughed together, loved together—and now it was over. Because Blade Forbes was an action man. Their honeymoon had been spent scuba diving and hang-gliding with long, warm nights of passionate love. He hardly knew what it was to be still. And she had loved that too along with everything else about him.

But how would such a man, hard, dynamic, with a zest for life that was unquenchable, cope with a wife who would be confined to a wheelchair by the time she was thirty and a hospital bed five years after that? Unable to move, breathe by herself?

The impersonal brutality of the stark medical facts came back to her as though she were reading them for the first time. The doctor's report she had been shown hadn't pulled any punches; indeed the clinical outline of the effects of the disease that was lying dormant in her body till it was matured enough to rear its head in a few years' time had seemed almost savage on that first reading. But then, how many ways were there to impart news like that? She twisted in the darkness, a pale slender figure in the shaft of moonlight from the uncurtained window.

The cold, typewritten report was engraved in her memory word for word; she only had to close her eyes for the small black letters to be there in all their severity. Her heart pounded as she ran over them again

in her mind, their message of a living death as hard
to take now as when she had first read it.

She had been right to leave Blade, she had. She
caught her breath on a sob of pain; she had had no
choice. But, oh—she gazed round the dark room
almost wildly—that didn't make it any easier.

CHAPTER TWO

'GOOD morning, Amy.' She stood transfixed, halfway out of the kitchen door, as Blade sauntered across the small restaurant after shutting the front door quietly behind him.

'What do you want?' she breathed softly, her eyes drinking in the sight of him even as her logic repudiated the thrill that had shot through her whole body.

'Lunch? If that's not too outrageous? I did assume this was a working restaurant?' The sarcasm was cold and biting and she blushed hotly as he seated himself at a table, his whole demeanour lazy and relaxed.

'Why are you here?' She moved to stand by his chair, her voice a low hiss.

'I am here to eat,' he said slowly, with exaggerated patience. 'You do remember that I do all the things a normal man does? Some with more enjoyment than others,' he finished silkily, his voice dark and rich and his eyes hard and mocking as she blushed hotly.

Thank goodness John would be away for another twenty-four hours yet; she had to get rid of Blade before that somehow.

'You know exactly what I mean,' she flashed back tightly. 'We said all that could be said yesterday——'

'We did not,' he said sharply. 'And please cut the naïve and stupid act because we both know that you are neither. We still have arrangements to make and matters to discuss. And my movements are my own affair, remember that, Amy. You have waived the right to question me in any way.'

'I see.' She glared at him angrily. 'It's the muscle-man approach, is it? Forcing your way in——'

'It was barely twenty-four hours ago that you accused me of being a bully in this very place,' he interrupted her coldly, his words falling like small pieces of ice into the heated atmosphere. 'I'd drop the insults if I were you, sweetheart. I don't like them and I have no intention of tolerating any more. Now, get the menu and do the job I assume the proprietor is paying you to do.'

His arrogance left her speechless and as she swung round, with a furious twist of her body that set the high silky ponytail at the back of her head swinging madly, she heard him laugh softly and the sound chilled her blood. There was no amusement, no mirth in the sound, just a callous, biting cruelty that brought all her fine body hairs upright in instinctive protection. Whatever game he was playing he wouldn't be able to keep it up forever and she would just have to put up with things for the moment, but *why* was he here? He'd said he despised her, that he felt nothing but contempt and scorn for her, so why was he back here this morning...? To torment her? She looked him full in the face as she placed the handwritten menu on the table in front of him, and the black eyes stared back at her, their expression unfathomable. Yes, that must be it. She wouldn't have thought he was capable of such pointless cruelty, but then she had never defied him before and after what he thought she had done maybe she shouldn't be surprised. Some men wouldn't have stopped at verbal abuse. And he still clearly intended to settle things with John in his own way.

'Thanks.' As he studied the menu she stood at his side, her eyes drawn to his bent head and a feeling of inexpressible emotion causing shivers of fear to flit down her spine in ever-increasing rhythm. His tawny brown hair gleamed richly with virile health in the May sunlight, his coal-black eyes with their thick, almost feminine lashes in impressive contrast. How often had she run her fingers through that mass of strong, coarse hair after a night of passion when she had felt as though even her toes were alive with sensual delight? He had been a magnificent lover. She forced her gaze up to stare blindly out of the window. Sensuous, erotic, but with a tender sensitivity to her own feelings that had caused the bond between them to strengthen and grow night by night. No wonder he didn't understand why she had left. If only she hadn't followed through on the impulse to visit Sandra that day. . .

'I'll have the soup, followed by an omelette, please.' She jumped visibly as he spoke and a dark frown creased his forehead. 'Daydreaming, Amy? I won't ask who's featured in them but for the moment would you concentrate on doing your job?' The tone was biting.

'You don't have to be so thoroughly unpleasant,' she said tightly as she wrote his order on the small notepad attached to her belt.

'You call this unpleasant?' he asked with a mocking, frosty amazement. 'You don't know the half, girl. But you will.' The dark eyes were pure granite. 'Oh, yes, you will.'

As she walked through to the kitchen a feeling of
incredible weariness had her hands shaking. Was all
this worth it? Perhaps it would be better to tell him?
To let him share in the agony with her rather than
bear it all alone? But then she remembered Sandra's
drawn, lined face, the sunken features and the still
young body already twisted into a caricature of an
old woman. Could she bear those eyes that had always
blazed with love and passion dulling with pity and
wretched, helpless misery? To have him look at her
each day as she slowly got worse, to see—— She
stopped her thoughts from the destructive path they
were following and straightened her back as hot rage
against the unfairness of it all flooded her system with
adrenalin.

Stop your whining, girl, she told herself fiercely as
the doorbell in the outer room signified more customers. One day, one hour at a time. She had realised
weeks ago that was the only way she was going to
bear the months and years ahead. If she looked into
the future she lost all her courage.

She took Blade's bowl of soup to his table before
she turned to the family that had seated themselves
in a corner across the other side of the room. All the
time she chatted with the two children and took the
parents' order she was aware of his gaze trained on
the back of her head even though she was turned from
him, but when she swung around and made her way
to the kitchen he was quietly eating a bread roll, his
dark eyes lazily surveying the peaceful scene outside
the window.

'What time do you finish work?' His tone was
brusque and his face expressionless as she served him

the freshly cooked Spanish omelette and baked potato
with a side salad.

'What?' Startled, she looked him straight in the eyes
and then wished she hadn't as the force of his gaze
pierced her to the spot.

'You heard what I said, Amy.' His voice was quiet
but with an undertone of iron that she knew from
old. How often she had heard him use that tone in
the past when he intended to get his own way. 'We
need to tie up a few loose ends so that the formalities
can progress smoothly. That's what you want, isn't
it? To be rid of me at the earliest opportunity?'

She dropped her eyes quickly, her face bleak. If he
only knew... She had never wanted or loved him as
much as she did now, when she was frightened and
lonely and desolately aware of what the future held.
To be able to lean on his strength, to rest in the
knowledge of his love, to be cushioned, at least in
part, by the comfort and support of his wealth... 'I
finish at eleven,' she said quietly. 'But I can meet you
tomorrow morning, if you like?'

'I'll be outside at eleven.' His tone brooked no ar-
gument and she nodded, still without looking at him,
before turning on her heel and seeking the sanctuary
of the steaming kitchen and Arthur's blunt normality.

All the rest of the afternoon and evening she func-
tioned on automatic, taking orders, smiling, engaging
in conversation while her mind ticked away on a completely different plane altogether.

When she had married Blade Forbes she had never
considered for a moment that it wouldn't be forever.
Her own parents had died in a car accident when she
was four years old and her sister, Sandra and herself

had been dispatched to different homes of distant re-
latives, Sandra to the wilds of Scotland and herself
into the heart of London. The two sisters hadn't been
close, the eight-year age-gap proving insurmountable
in view of Sandra's raging jealousy of her beautiful
baby sister, but Amy remembered crying as much for
her big sister as for her parents in the early days.

It wasn't until she had reached the age of sixteen
that she learnt Sandra had purposely repudiated all
contact in the intervening years, and after one shat-
tering, stunning visit to her married sister's home in
Scotland when she had quite literally had the door
banged in her face, she had determined to put Sandra
out of her life as successfully as her sister had apparently done with her. But... Amy shook her head
slowly as her thoughts travelled on. It hadn't been as
easy as that. Sandra was her only immediate family;
the same blood ran in their veins; she had wanted,
needed her love.

Weak and foolish, Amy thought grimly as she smil-
ingly served home-made steak and kidney pie to a little
Japanese couple with three cameras between them.
And how she had paid for the insecure feeling of in-
adequacy that had always dogged her footsteps. She
should have been satisfied with Blade, she shouldn't
have wanted more. What was a sister that she hadn't
seen for most of her life, after all?

The somewhat elderly aunt and uncle that she had
been homed with had caused her anxiety and in-
security, she knew that now after long, deep conver-
sations with Blade when she had poured out all her
doubts and fears. They had been fanatically strait-
laced, with a list of dos and don'ts that she had never

got the hang of, and her outstanding beauty had alarmed and repelled their austere, bigoted minds from the word go. She had been taught that she was undeserving and wayward, that her beauty was in some way shameful, from the first day that she had lived with them, and although something in her had always rebelled against such harsh reasoning some of the poison had got through.

But Blade had changed all that. She took a deep breath as her heart pounded painfully against her chest. He'd brought out all the old festering sores, held them up to the clean, purifying liquid of logic and reason, and in the process washed the wounds clean. And because of that she had felt strong enough to try and see Sandra again. And what she *had* seen and heard had appalled her.

Enough, Amy, enough, she told herself fiercely as she stared out into the dark night outside. An hour to go and you'll need all your wits to talk to Blade. Several cups of strong black coffee now and no more post-mortems.

When she emerged from the warm, cosy interior of the restaurant just over an hour later she thought for a moment that Blade hadn't come, and her stomach lurched churningly, whether in relief or disappointment she wasn't sure. And then she heard her name at the same time as he emerged from the shadows across the other side of the road.

'Where's your car?' she asked weakly, as he reached her side. He was dressed casually in jeans and black leather jacket and he'd turned her legs to water.

'Quite safe.' His voice was mocking with a hard bite of cruelty. 'I thought we would walk the short distance to your lodgings.'

'You know where I live?' she asked in alarm.

'Of course.' He looked down at her, slender and waiflike against his hard masculine bulk. 'The private detective I hired to find you is both thorough and discreet and excellent at his job.'

'He would be,' she answered dully. Blade only tolerated the best.

'Come along.' He took her arm in a firm grip as he turned her in the direction of Mrs Cox's little guest house, and although the contact was brief the heat from his fingers seemed to burn her arm. She had jerked away before she could check herself and as his body stiffened at her side she cursed the gesture. It would only make him angrier. It did.

'I'm not a disease that's fatal on contact,' he said cuttingly, 'and another little move like that and I warn you now I won't be responsible for my actions. Understand?'

'I didn't mean——'

'I know what you *meant*.' The hard voice was inflexible. 'And I'm quite aware that I'm not the person you wish to be with, but as I'm here and he isn't I suggest you act accordingly.'

They walked the length of the street in silence and she began to feel almost faint with a mixture of terrified foreboding and lack of food. She hadn't been able to force anything past the huge lump in her throat all day and she hadn't eaten her evening meal last night. *He* had eaten the meal at lunchtime with every appearance of relaxed enjoyment, she thought resentfully as they turned into the quiet unlit lane that led eventually to the small row of cottages in which her lodgings were situated. But then, why shouldn't he? she asked herself honestly. What a mess this was, what a hopeless, terrifying mess.

'Now then.' As he swung her round she had no idea of his intention, but as his arms closed round her in an embrace that had her arms pinned at her sides and her head thrown back he took her lips in a brutal punishing kiss that spoke of his fury more eloquently than any words could have done.

She tried to move her head, to break the hold of his mouth on hers, but his force was relentless and she was trapped as effortlessly as a tiny mouse between the paws of a big black cat. The familiar smell of him filled her nostrils and in spite of the knowledge that this was intended as a cruel exercise in submission she found herself responding to his touch in the old way, her body eager for any contact with the man she loved beyond life. He sensed her capitulation immediately, his mouth softening fractionally as his hands moved up and over her straining breasts, caressing her thoroughly and completely before he moved away in a hard movement that almost threw her from him. The whole embrace couldn't have lasted more than a couple of minutes but as she stood swaying in the darkness, her eyes fixed on his in mute appeal, she felt as though they had made love for hours.

'I don't believe it.' There was contempt and raw scorn in his voice along with something else she couldn't recognise, something almost bordering on pain. 'You can kiss me like that after all you've done. Who the hell are you, Amy, *what* are you?' His eyes

were dark and glittering in the single shaft of moonlight filtering down between the newly leafed branches
of the huge oak trees bordering the lane. 'I expected
you to fight me, to object—something!' He was furiously, bitterly angry, she reflected dully as she watched
his contorted face in the shadows, more angry than
she had ever seen him. 'I thought I'd met the lot in
my time but you sure as hell take the biscuit! Even
the trashiest whore wouldn't...'

He was still speaking as she slid into a dead faint
at his feet, her hair fanning out in a golden halo under
her head and her face deathly white in the still night.

She came round slowly, her head jangling with a
thousand nightmarish images, to find herself held
close to his chest as he knelt beside her on the thick
grass of the small verge. 'Blade...?' She couldn't
speak very well; her brain seemed to know what it
wanted to say but her tongue wouldn't obey.

'Keep still.' There was a look on his face that caused
the blood to pound violently in her ears, a piercing,
haunting cry of burning hunger, unmitigated rage,
dark fear and a terrible expectation of she knew not
what. 'You fainted. Keep still.'

'I fainted?' Her lips seemed wooden she reflected
dazedly. 'I've never done that before.'

'No.' He seemed about to speak and then the words
were stilled as he surveyed her through veiled eyes in
which all emotion was suddenly blanked. 'Have you
got something to tell me, Amy?'

'Tell you?' She tried to move away but his arms
were rigid. 'I don't understand.'

He swore, softly but with deadly intensity, before
lifting her up into his arms as he stood upright. 'Let

me put it like this,' he said grimly as he stood for a
moment before striding down the lane in the direction
of the lights in the distance. 'It is not unusual, in
certain circumstances, for a woman to pass out round
about the time of three months. Do I have to go on?'

'What?' She twisted so sharply in his hold that he
almost dropped her. 'You think I'm—you do, don't
you?'

'It wouldn't be the first time that a woman has left
her husband for another man and in the first flush of
unbridled passion got a little more than she had bar-
gained for,' he said, with a terrible lack of expression
in his voice and face.

'Put me down, Blade.' Her voice was faint, more
from the intoxicating sensation of being held in his
arms again than the import of his words. Her head
was muzzy and her legs felt like jelly but she knew
she had to stand on her own two feet again before she
disgraced herself a second time. The temptation to
wind her arms tightly round his neck and kiss his face
and throat was fast becoming too strong to resist, and
she could just imagine his reaction. It was clear from
what he had said that he had intended the kiss as a
punishment and lesson in obedience; he hadn't expected her either to enjoy or tolerate it. He was
probably very disappointed his chastisement hadn't
worked as he'd envisaged, she thought miserably.

'Can you walk?' Even as he spoke he had placed
her on *terra firma* again, moving back a pace swiftly
as though the contact with her body had repelled him.

He loathed her, she thought painfully. Loathed and
hated her. 'I'm not expecting a baby, Blade.' How she

kept her voice steady she would never know. 'There is no possibility of that at all.'

'I see.' He surveyed her coldly, eyes narrowed and hands thrust deep in the pockets of his jacket. 'Well, at least you kept enough sanity to take care of that side of things.'

'I don't want to discuss it.' As she went to walk he stepped forward abruptly to block her path, his eyes icy.

'Don't you indeed?' He shook his head slowly. 'You know, your sheer effrontery amazes me. What happened to the happy innocent girl I married, Amy?'

'She's dead.' The words passed her lips before she had even thought about them, coming straight from the heart, and something in her tone of voice must have set the antennae buzzing again because his eyes searched her face slowly and consideringly, their inky depths thoughtful, before he took her arm and indicated that they continue walking.

'Now what makes me think that the course of true love is not running as smoothly as you would have liked?' he asked coldly, with bitterly raw cynicism. 'What's the problem, Amy? Did lover-boy prefer having you as an extra little titbit now and again rather than you camping on his doorstep?'

She glared at him without answering as Mrs Cox's small detached cottage drew nearer.

'Or maybe the appeal of being a working girl again in the big bad world is less than attractive?' He looked down at her steadily, his eyes veiled.

'Can't you just leave things alone?' she asked tightly. 'Accept——'

'By "things" I take it you mean you?' He smiled
coldly. 'You would like that, wouldn't you: to be able
to finish my chapter in your life as though this were
all an abstract exercise? But it isn't and we aren't.
You are still my wife—*my wife*, Amy.' The emphasis
and intonation of his words were exactly as spoken
in the dream, and as a slow shiver crept down her
spine she gazed up at him with naked fear in her eyes.

'Do I frighten you?' They had reached the cottage
now and he leant back against the post of the garden
gate as he swung it open for her, his stance lazy and
laconic and his face cruel. 'You'd be wise to fear me,
Amy. People have feared me for far less than you have
done.'

'You don't scare me,' she lied bravely as she lifted
her chin a fraction. 'And I don't like threats.'

'Then take it as a warning,' he drawled smoothly
as his gaze held her eyes, their blueness dark and
velvety in the moonlight. 'One that you can pass on
to interested parties. I understand John is due home
tomorrow.' The last sentence had been arctic cold, his
voice chilling.

He had turned and walked off down the lane before
she could react and she felt a moment's deep thankfulness that he hadn't seen the relief on her face. He
still thought this was something to do with poor John,
then? If she could just get through the next few days
without betraying herself he would have to leave soon.
His empire needed him at the helm and he couldn't
afford to be away for long, besides which this place
would drive him mad. She would have smiled to
herself if her heart hadn't been so raw and bleeding.
The swelling moorlands, deep wooded valleys, rolling

hills with their trickling pure streams and crystal-clear
waterfalls that spelt peace and sanctuary to her would
be an enigma to the man she had married. His place
was in the cut and thrust of the razor-sharp business
world he inhabited. The hectic lifestyle and cynical,
sceptical people he dealt with every day were what he
knew. Her quiet backwater with its stolid, unexcitable
Yorkshire folk who were the salt of the earth couldn't
be more different. He'd soon tire of all this and
then——

'One more thing, Amy.' She started violently as he
reappeared at her side, dark eyes glittering hotly. 'I've
got all the time it takes.' It was as though he had read
her mind and she stared at him, with the garden gate
a small wooden barrier between them, as he smiled
sardonically. 'I'm in no rush to get back to London,
and this is a beautiful part of the world. Now go in
and rest; you look as though you're going to pass out
again.' He was mocking, taunting her! She kept her
thoughts hidden as the black gaze raked her face.

'The last three months have been a little—troublesome. I could do with a nice relaxing holiday about
now. What do you think?' he finished silkily.

'I think you're lying through your back teeth,' she
said angrily. 'In all the time I've known you you have
never, *ever*, had a "nice relaxing holiday" of any description. It would kill you——'

'Ah, but then that's the crux of the matter, my
sweet.' There was no mockery in the deep cold voice
now. 'You haven't really "known" me at all, have
you? A whirlwind courtship and within months you
were a blushing bride. You have no idea really of what
makes me tick. If you had, you would never have had

the temerity to walk out on me with another man.'
The icy threat in his words was unmistakable. 'And
don't make the mistake of thinking that I'm staying
here because I care in any way. I've told you before,
I don't.' He eyed her cuttingly. 'But you are my
property as far as I see it and no one, *no one* steals
what is mine.'

'Your property?' For the first time since he had
come back in her life undiluted burning rage swept
all the darkness out of her mind. 'How dare you say
that?'

As she raised her hand to strike him he moved
swiftly, grasping her upraised hand in an iron hold at
the same time as pushing her backwards while he
opened the gate with his legs, joining her in the small
front garden before she could draw breath.

'You don't like my terminology?' he said tauntingly. 'Well, how would you describe yourself, then?'

'I'm your wife, not your property,' she said hotly
as she struggled against the sheer hard bulk of his
body. 'How dare you say that, how——?'

'Ah, so you've remembered at last.' As his lips descended on hers for the second time that night she
began to fight, really fight, with her arms and legs
kicking and writhing in desperate panic as she twisted
her head this way and that to avoid his searching
mouth. She heard him swear once, softly, as her foot
made brief harsh contact with his shin-bone, and then
he had pinned her arms at her sides as effortlessly as
though she were a child, moving her backwards into
the shadows of a gnarled old lilac tree that was
scenting the cool night air with its heady perfume.

'You need to be taught a lesson, my girl,' he said thickly.

She knew, even as she continued to struggle, that it was a hopeless battle. It wasn't really him she was fighting after all, there might have been some hope of success if it were, but it was her own weakness where he was concerned that was sending her whole system into hyper-drive.

His mouth was warm and firm and sensual on hers and she knew instinctively he was seeking to break down her resistance with persuasion rather than force. And to what end? she thought desperately. He didn't really want her any more, he had made it perfectly clear that he considered her damaged goods. No, this was a cruel revenge of the worst kind because once it was over he would leave her without a second thought. But that was what she wanted, surely? her mind ground on as his hands and mouth worked their magic on her shaking body. She'd made the decision three months ago that she had to leave and face the fury and hatred such an apparently motiveless action would bring down on her head; she couldn't back out now, she just couldn't. But she hadn't envisaged this sweet torture, not in her wildest nightmares.

'I could kill you for what you've done...' His voice was a thick frantic murmur against the smooth white column of her throat as he groaned her name before devouring her lips again in a kiss that was endless.

She was powerless to hide the shudders that were coursing through her body, the touch, the taste of him was intoxicatingly delicious and she felt drunk with the pleasure his lovemaking induced. She knew she ought to continue to fight him, that it was madness

to wind her arms round his neck and return his kisses
in heated desire, but nevertheless that was exactly what
she found herself doing.

The light jacket she had been wearing was at her
feet—how it had got there she didn't know—and now
his hands were on the silky skin beneath her open
blouse, his fingers gentle but firm as they moulded
the soft fullness of her breasts. There was a moment
of startled protest as his head lowered to take possession of what his hands had found, and then she
was lost completely and utterly in the sensations his
lips drew.

She loved him, so much, but she couldn't—
couldn't . . .

'Amy?' Mrs Cox's voice cut into the moment like
a rapier-sharp blade. 'Is that you out there, Amy? I
heard a noise . . .' They were hidden from sight behind
the overgrown foliage in the small front garden, but
as Blade stiffened and his hands and mouth froze Amy
felt a deluge of icy water wash through her veins.

She glanced down at her dishevelled clothing. What
on earth had she been thinking of! What she'd been
thinking of moved quickly, his voice light and pleasant
with just the right touch of embarrassed warmth in
it to appeal to an old woman's motherly instincts. 'It
is Amy, Mrs . . . Cox?' Blade moved out of the shadows
and walked a few steps into the shaft of light from
the open front door. 'I walked Amy home from the
restaurant, Mrs Cox. We were just saying good-night.'

'Is that right?' Mrs Cox's normally slow Yorkshire
drawl was tight with suspicion. 'Where is she, then?'

'Here, Mrs Cox.' Amy moved out of the shadows as she pretended to tidy her hair, her clothing now in place.

'You know him?' The plump little woman gestured towards Blade's large masculine figure that dwarfed her by a good foot, looking for all the world like a fat little ruffled hen prepared to face an intruder that had threatened one of her chicks.

'He's an old friend, Mrs Cox.' Amy's cheeks were burning so fiercely they hurt and she was careful to stand just out of the light. 'Just popped down from London.'

'Now that isn't quite right, Mrs Cox.' Blade's voice was infinitely pleasant and warm and the expression he had stitched on to his face made Amy want to hit him, hard. It was one of innocent candour and honest guilelessness, his eyes wide with ingenuous frankness and a desire to please. Amy had never trusted him less. 'In actual fact I am Amy's husband, albeit estranged. We separated three months ago,' he added with just enough unspoken regret to make it clear who had left whom.

'I see. Well, that's none of my business,' Mrs Cox said stiffly, but even from her place in the shadows Amy could see that the little woman's face had mellowed and her bright button eyes were a good deal warmer as they held Blade's dark glance. He's done it again, Amy thought with equal amazement and resentment. Melted all opposition with just two well chosen sentences and a good deal of old traditional charm. Mrs Cox wasn't really going to fall for this line of artless simplicity, was she? It appeared she was. 'Perhaps you'd like to come in and have a cup of tea before you leave?' the little Yorkshirewoman continued quietly. 'I've just made a pot.'

'That's really very kind of you.' As he followed Mrs Cox into the house he turned once at the threshold, allowing Amy to precede him into the hall, and as she glanced at his face it was as hard as iron.

What was all this about? Amy thought helplessly. He had never willingly drunk tea in his life, preferring strong black coffee, and she knew him well enough to know that he never did anything on impulse. But of course... As she sat down by the heavily banked coal fire in the small sitting-room and listened to Blade charm Mrs Cox out of the trees, the reality of what he was about came to her in a blinding flash. This was her bolthole, her refuge, and he wanted to destroy it for her. He had spoken of punishment, retribution, hadn't he? He was going to let Mrs Cox, and everyone else who had befriended her in the small village, know that she had left him for another man after a few months of marriage. This was a small community and a highly moral one with certain codes and rules that were adhered to as strictly now as at the beginning of the century. She would still be treated politely, with the well-mannered courtesy that was an integral part of village life here, but Blade would have stamped her as 'that' type of woman, on a par with her predecessor at the restaurant who had run off with her lover and left a desolate husband and children. And in a few days, maybe one or two, he would leave. *Fait accompli!*

It came to her, as she sat there in the dim warm light that reflected the glowing fire's flickering shadows on the old, highly polished furniture, that

all this wasn't going to be as straightforward as she
had imagined. And the thought terrified her because
he mustn't, he *mustn't,* find out the truth. She would
do anything, anything at all, to prevent that.

She glanced at his hands as they rested on the old
leather arms of the chair. Solid gold watch on one
tanned wrist, the signet ring inset with a single large
diamond in one corner that she had given him on their
wedding day, all the trappings of fabulous wealth that
had surrounded her from their first meeting.

But all the opulence, the rich affluence, had been
no protection against the long hand of fate. It had
reached out through all Blade's hard-won assets, the
cleverly amassed fortune, and touched her with its icy
fingers.

That had been one of the things Sandra had snarled
at her that day, she remembered with a painful
thudding of her heart, as she pictured her sister's
twisted angry face in her mind.

'You thought you had it all, didn't you? A
millionaire and a handsome one to boot.' Sandra's
voice had been shaking with rage and bitterness. 'But
you've got nothing now, little sister, nothing at all,
in the end you're just as naked and cold as the rest
of us. Your looks will mean nothing once the disease
strikes. Look at me, have a good hard look. This is
you in a few years' time. And he won't be able to do
anything, if that's what you're thinking. All the money
in the world can't. I know, I've asked.'

Sandra's tormented face had glared at her with raw
frustration in every pore. 'He thought he was getting
a beautiful little doll to show off to all his jet-setting
friends and instead you are going to be a millstone

round his neck! That's really very funny when you think about it. Can you see the joke, Amy? Can you?'

'You're sick in more than body, Sandra,' Amy had whispered faintly as she stared back into the maddened eyes. If it weren't for the fact that her sister was a prisoner in the wheelchair, she was sure she would have leapt at her face like a small demented goblin. As it was, her hands were gripping the arms of the wheelchair in a claw motion that was infinitely chilling.

'What do you know about it?' Sandra had screamed bitterly. 'You were always the favoured one, so pretty, so perfect. You've had a charmed life so far with everything going your way. Not like me!'

'No, I haven't.' Amy had stood for a moment poised on the threshold of Sandra's room in the old terraced house in the heart of Glasgow, her hand clutching the chilling medical report Sandra had given her a few minutes before, her sister having watched with fiendish satisfaction as she absorbed the portent of the doctor's statement. 'I had a miserable childhood with Aunt Alice and Uncle Julian. The only real happiness I've known has been since I've met Blade.'

'Well, excuse me if I don't shed any tears for you.' There had been something truly malignant in Sandra's dark eyes. 'I hate you, Amy. I've always hated you. I shall die hating you.'

She had left then, stunned and broken, still clutching the damning evidence in nerveless hands, and it had been a miracle she had ever reached London safely the way she had been feeling. She couldn't remember the journey at all.

She had stumbled into the beautiful city garden, her face white and stiff and her whole body shaking, and sat for hours as her tired mind screamed back and forth as she tried to come to terms with what she had read. *In a few years she was going to die.*

She shook her head blindly. Slowly, very slowly, Sandra had emphasised. Day by day, week by week, month by month, her strength would ebb and her muscles wither as her body gave up the fight to go on. She was going to die. She had ripped the report into tiny tiny pieces but had found each word was imprinted on the pages of her mind.

Blade's deep voice suddenly cut into her thoughts as he replied to something Mrs Cox had said, and she came back to the present with a little jerk of her body, amazed to find herself in the small room with its old heavy furniture and glowing fire.

Yes. She would do anything, *anything*, to keep the truth from him even if it meant he would leave this place hating the very sound of her name.

CHAPTER THREE

SHE had half expected Blade to do a repeat of the previous day's fiasco, but when he didn't appear the following lunchtime, far from being reassuring, it turned Amy into a veritable bag of nerves. Every jingle of the old doorbell, every muffled male voice, and she shot over to the kitchen door or swung round in the restaurant until by the time she was ready to leave at eleven her head was pounding as though she had been hit by a sledgehammer.

As she stepped out into the quiet village street just after eleven the cool sweet air, redolent of large open spaces and high empty skies, was wonderfully soothing to her overheated metabolism.

She stood for a moment on the narrow stone step and breathed deeply with her eyes shut. As she opened them again two events happened simultaneously. A large dark figure detached itself from the shadows and began walking towards her at the same time as John called her name from his cheerful little Morris Minor parked a few yards down the road. 'Amy? Over here.'

She felt for a moment as though she were caught up in a play, a macabre twisted play. Blade had frozen in mid-stride, his eyes flashing from her horrified face to the car partially hidden by the darkness, and then he moved like lightning, reaching the car before she could even pull herself together sufficiently to move.

'The elusive John Davies, I presume?' His voice had all the warmth of cold steel. 'Let me introduce myself. I am Blade Forbes, Amy's husband.' He wrenched open the driver's door with such force that Amy wouldn't have been surprised if it had come off in his hand. 'I think there is a little matter we need to discuss, Mr Davies, if you would like to step out of the car.'

'Leave him alone, Blade.' She had reached his side now, her frightened eyes taking in John's startled face as he peered upwards at Blade, whose chiselled features were icy with rage and hate.

'Leave him alone?' Blade growled softly. 'Later, much later, my sweet unfaithful little spouse. Now, Mr Davies.' He swung back to focus directly on John. 'Are you going to leave this car of your own free will or do I have to drag you out?'

'I have to say neither option appeals,' John murmured wryly as he stared up at Blade's wide powerful six-foot frame, 'but if you insist, you'll have to pass those crutches in the back seat.'

'What?' For the first time that she could remember Amy saw Blade momentarily nonplussed as he glanced from John's round, bespectacled pale face to the pair of steel crutches lying in the back of the car.

'The crutches,' John repeated patiently. 'Owing to an unexpected nosedive off a mountain in Spain some months ago I'm afraid those things are essential, so if you wouldn't mind...?'

'I don't believe this.' Blade flicked his head at Amy furiously. 'Is this guy for real?'

'It's as he said,' Amy said quietly, as she swallowed back the panic. 'John was living in Spain, he's a writer, and he went on a walking expedition into the mountains with some friends. There was an accident——'

'I don't want his life story,' Blade interrupted bitingly. 'Can he walk?'

'Yes, I can walk.' John's voice was tinged with acerbity, which was unusual for him, Amy reflected agitatedly. She hoped he wasn't going to pick this moment to step out of character. He was normally so mild-mannered, so easygoing...

'Then I still want you out of the car.' As Blade reached down and opened the back door to pass the crutches to John, Amy's stomach took a crazy dive into her feet. What was he going to do? He wouldn't attack John now, would he? Not knowing John was injured? She glanced round her frantically but the dark street was quite deserted.

'Right.' It had taken John a few seconds to manipulate himself from the interior of the car and she could tell he didn't like it. His pale face was flushed and pink and his five-foot-eight frame fairly bristling with dislike as he stared straight into Blade's furious countenance. 'What's this all about?'

'What's this all...?' Blade's voice trailed away as he stared at the smaller man propped up with the crutches under each arm. 'Oh, you English. What the hell do you think it's about? A small matter of adultery, or maybe that has slipped your mind.' His teeth were grinding together in his rage. 'Or are you going to deny it?'

'Deny it?' John's round pleasant face flushed a deeper shade of red. 'Do I take it you are accusing me of sleeping with Amy?'

'Got it in one,' Blade said viciously. 'And believe me, if it weren't for the fact that you are obviously unable to defend yourself——'

'I can see now why Amy felt it necessary to leave you,' John said tightly. 'I'm only amazed it took her all of three months to find out she'd made such a bad mistake. How dare you——?'

'How dare you?' Amazingly, as John got angrier and angrier Blade became more calm and composed, his dark satirical features setting into cold ironical lines and his black eyes cynically cool. 'I rather think in the circumstances that's my line, don't you?' He smiled chillingly. 'How long have you known my wife?' The last two words were stressed, very slightly, with biting contempt.

'Years,' John answered irritably.

'Could you be a little more precise?' Blade eyed the smaller man expressionlessly, his voice dripping ice.

'We met when Amy was doing A levels,' John said testily. 'Some of her college friends had a flat next to mine and in the evenings we all ate together. Amy moved in with them after a time when things became impossible for her at home. We found we had a lot in common,' he added with spitefulness that was unusual to him. Amy glanced at him in horror and shut her eyes for a split-second as she drew in air between her teeth. What was the matter with him? she asked herself silently. Had he a death wish or something?

'How cosy.' Blade's rapier-sharp gaze switched to Amy and then back to John's defiant face. 'And do I presume your relationship blossomed in the normal way?'

'That would depend on what you consider normal,' John said tightly. I——'

'John lived with a girlfriend at that time,' Amy put in desperately, 'a very nice girl. We got on really well——'

Blade silenced the flow with one fiery glance before turning to John again. 'And do I take it the girlfriend has long since been history?'

'I've lived in Spain for the last three years and my private life is nothing to do with you,' John said angrily as he drew himself up to his full height, his chin thrust out aggressively. 'Amy is a dear friend of mine and I was honoured that it was me she came to when she left you.'

'Were you indeed?' For a moment Amy thought Blade was going to leap on the smaller man, crutches and all.

Why are you saying all this, John? she asked silently. Tell him you tried to persuade me to go back and sort it all out. Tell him you were against me hiding like this, especially when I couldn't give you a good reason for leaving Blade. Tell him——

'Yes, I was,' John continued. 'And I can understand a little better now why she was so terrified and upset when she came to me. What on earth did you do to her, anyway?'

Amy anticipated Blade's reaction just in time, flinging herself in front of John as Blade moved forward, his eyes murderous. She should have told John the real reason why she left, she thought frantically as she looked up into Blade's blazing eyes. But she hadn't wanted his pity or compassion to weaken her and bring on the bouts of self-pity at a time when

she needed to be strong. And so she had just said the
marriage wasn't working and John, being John,
hadn't probed. But it had been a mistake. A bad
mistake, she realised now as John spoke just behind
her.

'I can look after myself, Amy; get out of the way.'

'Blade—please.' She put both hands on Blade's
chest as the black eyes flicked over both of them.
'Please...' She didn't know quite what she was
pleading for but the fear in her eyes spoke volumes
to the tall, hard man in front of her.

Blade held her glance for a long piercingly taut
minute and then, as the stiff body relaxed slightly, she
felt faint with relief. 'To hell with it, with you both,'
he said quietly, a curious lack of expression in his
voice. 'If *he* is what you want——'

He swung round sharply and walked down the road,
pausing only briefly as John called after him, his voice
angry, 'It isn't what you think, man!' So John had
noticed the crucifying agony in Blade's eyes that
second as he turned away too, Amy thought faintly,
as the pain in her heart stopped her breath. What had
she done? *What had she done?*

'Amy, I don't understand any of this.' John had
remained standing with her, silent and still in the dark
night for long minutes, and now he turned to her, his
round pleasant face troubled and flushed. 'Why did
you leave him? Why wasn't it working? Did he hit
you, is that it?'

'No.' Amy shook her head weakly as she leant back
against the stone wall bordering a front garden. 'But
I can't talk about it, John. I had to leave. I can't go
back. That's it.'

'OK, OK.' He shook his head slowly. 'But you sure picked one hell of a guy to tangle with. He's trouble, Amy, with a capital T. I don't like him.'

You don't understand, she thought blindly as she shut her eyes against the concern and worry in John's face. You couldn't even begin to understand him. He's warm and tender and funny and everything any woman could hope for in a man. Trouble? Maybe. But that came with the package——

'I'll take you home.' John's voice was flat now and as he levered himself back into the car she felt a moment's deep guilt that she had involved him in all this. He had enough troubles of his own with the painful and exhausting treatment he was undergoing to get back the full use of his legs. That was why he had reacted to Blade's hostility in the way he had. Normally John was the first one to pour oil on troubled waters; she had never known him to react so violently before.

She climbed in the passenger seat quietly, the guilt rising again as she took in the specially adapted controls of the car. John hated his helplessness, the vulnerability that the confrontation with Blade had exposed in all its rawness. She should never have come here, never have stayed.

As she got ready for bed an hour later she stood for long minutes looking at herself in the full-length mirror on the front of the small wardrobe in her room. Heart-shaped face, large violet-blue heavily lashed eyes, small straight nose and a traditional English 'peaches and cream' complexion. She couldn't be less like Sandra if she had tried, she thought painfully. Her sister's somewhat square face was framed by thick

dark hair that hadn't the smallest natural kink in it
and her dark brown eyes made her the very image of
their father. But she wouldn't think of Sandra now.
A flood of churning bitterness seared over her heart.
If only she hadn't thought of her at all, given into
that crazy impulse to try and heal the rift between
them. Because of that she had broken Blade's heart
and killed everything that was good between them.
She couldn't bear this agony, she couldn't... Her face
was still wet with tears as she drifted, hours later, into
a troubled, restless sleep populated with changing
nightmarish images that weaved and coiled into her
mind over and over again.

She didn't like Sundays. At least each weekday and
especially Saturday she was kept busy at the restaurant from lunchtime until late at night, and with
John providing moral support when needed the days
didn't seem too bad. But John always visited his
mother some fifty miles away on Sundays and without
his friendly presence she had too much time to think.
   She sighed heavily to herself as she lay in bed the
Sunday morning after Blade's re-entry into her life,
watching a dancing beam of sunlight on the wall opposite. It had been three days since that devastating
confrontation outside the restaurant and she hadn't
seen Blade since, although she knew from John that
he was still around. John had made it his business to
find out that Blade was renting a small cottage on the
outskirts of the village. 'He's taken a three-month
contract,' John had said grimly, his mild blue eyes
worried and angry. 'What do you think he's playing
at, Amy?' She had shrugged slowly, shaking her head.

She wished she knew. She really did. But whatever it was it wouldn't be to her advantage, that much she was sure of.

She wandered downstairs in time to eat her breakfast with Mrs Cox, a little routine the older woman appreciated being, Amy suspected, quite lonely most of the time, and it was as she was eating the fluffy scrambled eggs on toast that she asked the question that had just occurred to her, the answer to which made her wish she had kept her mouth shut.

'You haven't seen anything of Blade over the last couple of days, have you?' she asked the small, stout woman quietly as Mrs Cox refilled the big pottery teapot with hot water.

'Your husband?' Mrs Cox eyed her carefully. 'Not since the morning after the night I met him, lass. Why?'

'He came to see you the next morning?' Amy asked faintly, hoping against hope Mrs Cox would say they had met by accident in the street, shopping, anything...

'Aye, lass.' Mrs Cox's eyes were steady and direct on hers. 'And I must say I've never been partial to Americans but that one——' she nodded to herself as she poured her fifth cup of tea of the morning '—he's all right.' The rebuke was mild but Amy still felt it like a slap in the face. How could she tell the older woman she agreed completely with her analysis? Blade was all right. He was more than all right.

'What did he want?' she asked carefully, but Mrs Cox shook her head gently, her gaze unwavering on Amy's flushed face.

'Now I think that was betwixt me and him, lovey,
don't you?' she answered steadily. 'I don't interfere
in no one's affairs, as you know. You ask him when
you see him.' There was no malice in her landlady's
voice, nor even accusation, but Amy knew better than
to pursue the conversation. And she would have respected the other woman's honesty in other circumstances, but just at the moment it made her want to
shake the poor inoffensive soul.

'I might not be seeing him again,' she answered
quietly and it was a second later, as though to prove
her wrong, that the front doorbell rang imperiously.

'Is she in, Mrs Cox?' She heard his voice in the hall
and swallowed a piece of toast so quickly it lodged in
her throat like a bone. She was gulping tea in an effort
to clear it, eyes streaming, when Blade strolled lazily
into the small sunlit room.

'Good morning.' He made no attempt to smile or
lighten the situation in any way as his eyes fastened
on to hers like lasers, and she saw he was still im-
mersed in the rage and fury that had tightened the
big powerful body into a coiled spring and turned the
dark face stony.

'I was just saying to Mrs Cox I thought I might not
see you again,' she answered at last when her choking
had finished.

He eyed her for a long moment before replying and
Amy shivered as Mrs Cox joined them and his face
became bland and pleasant. There was still something
flowing beneath that was toxic. 'Wishful thinking?'
His manner was genial and Mrs Cox clucked amiably
as she bustled away to fetch an extra cup from the
kitchen, but the coal-black eyes were as hard as iron

and Amy knew his comment had been as sharp as barbed wire, the message contained therein for her ears alone.

'I'm taking you out for a drive and a pub lunch,' he said softly after half a minute had ticked by in total silence. Mrs Cox was a long time in returning with the cup; Amy fancied the elderly woman thought she was being tactful! 'If you have made other arrangements, cancel them.'

The hard arrogance brought every defensive instinct she possessed into immediate life and she stiffened slowly, her face hostile. 'I'm sorry, Blade.' She tried to make her voice as bland as she could but it was difficult with every nerve and sinew in her body stretched as tight as a drum. 'I'm afraid I can't—— '

'I apologise, I obviously haven't made myself clear,' he said silkily. 'I wasn't *inviting* you, Amy, I was telling you what I expect you to do.'

'Now, just you look here——'

He cut off her angry response with just a narrowing of his eyes and a slight lifting of his chin, but suddenly the striking animalistic power of the man was intensely fierce and much to her disgust she felt herself shrink back against her chair as though she were a tiny creature confronted with a violent and predatory hunter. *He frightened her*! The thought amazed and shocked her more than she would have thought possible. But this wasn't the Blade she had known through their brief courtship and the first heady days of marriage. This man, with his sensual and compelling authority, was dreadfully remote, the saturnine features cold and analytical and the dark eyes that had always been warm and glowing with love terrifyingly unfathomable in their austere blackness.

'Do you like it here?' As the piercing gaze left her white face and travelled slowly round the small cluttered room, she could see both bewilderment and curiosity flare briefly in the hard face.

A mental picture of the fabulous home she had shared with him in London flashed briefly into her mind. Parquet floors covered with precious Chinese silk rugs, exquisite antiques arranged beautifully for both comfort and effect, wonderful oil paintings and Olympic-sized indoor swimming pool and overall the delicate, heady perfume of hot-house flowers that were replaced daily by one of the live-in servants long before the rest of the household was awake. It was the profusion of flowers that had impressed her the most when she had first visited his home, she remembered, and after they had married she had protested at the unnecessary renewing of still perfect blooms. His reply was crystal-clear in her mind and something she had returned to time and time again in the last three months.

'It pleases me,' he had said, taking both her hands in his and kissing the tip of her nose lightly. 'They should go while they are still perfect, before any blemish mars their beauty and they become painful to look at. I don't like to watch them die or fade, Amy. Decay revolts me.'

At the time she had been struck by the darkness in his face and had passed the moment off quickly, seeking only to comfort and soothe, but then weeks later, when she had seen Sandra, his words had returned with such vividness that she had been physically sick.

'Yes, I like it,' she answered quietly. 'It's a far cry from your home but it has its own charm and——'

'I didn't mean it like that,' he answered sharply. 'I wasn't comparing in any way, putting the place down. It's just that you seemed to love London so much, the bright lights, the fast pace——'

'Maybe I've grown up,' she said simply, veiling her eyes as the glittering gaze moved discerningly over her face.

'It was your home too, you know.' His voice was soft now, and very deep. 'Just as much as mine.'

'No, it never was.' She didn't want to hurt or antagonise, but the palatial house in a quiet, discreet London suburb had never felt like home. 'It was beautiful and I felt privileged to live there, but there was none of me in it. Everything had been organised, arranged, for years before I came into your life and still continued to be when I joined you, even down to the last bowl of flowers.'

'If you felt like that, why didn't you *say*?' There was a stricken look in his eyes that suddenly made her feel horribly guilty.

'Because it wasn't important at the time,' she said quickly, 'and still isn't really. I shouldn't have said anything, I'm sorry.' She shook her head distractedly, her soft blonde hair that she had left loose on her shoulders glowing like molten gold. 'It was a wonderful home, I was very lucky——'

'To hell with your luck!' There was a ragged note to his voice that brought her head snapping up but his face was unreadable, cold and remote. 'I didn't want you to consider yourself *lucky*, for crying out loud. I thought we loved each other, that we had a marriage——' He stopped abruptly, turning from her in one violent movement to stride the two paces to the window where he stood with his back to her gazing out into the wilderness of a garden.

'I know what you're thinking, lad——' Amy had quite forgotten about Mrs Cox, but now as the little woman joined them with the requisite cup and saucer she was immensely glad of the diversion. 'Jungle, isn't it?'

Blade turned quickly, the mask he was so adept at putting in place fixed and smiling. 'A little overgrown, shall we say?' he suggested with a quirk of one dark eyebrow.

'Needs must.' The small Yorkshirewoman was nothing if not colloquial. 'Since Mr Cox died it's been enough to cope with the house and the odd guest. I can't do with setting the garden in order. A body can only do so much.' She nodded her grey head in confirmation of her words.

'I could spend an hour or two out there, if you like?' Blade suggested lightly. 'I enjoy the odd bit of gardening and as long as you keep the coffee coming hot and strong we'll call it quits.'

He enjoyed the odd bit of gardening? Amy almost choked on the words. To her knowledge in Blade's eyes a fork was something you ate with and a spade was a character in a deck of cards. He didn't even confer with the top gardeners he employed periodically to keep the immaculate grounds surrounding his home in pristine condition.

'That's if Amy has no objection, of course,' he continued smoothly, turning a blank face to her as he smiled silkily.

No objection? She would have liked to be able to spit her objections into his face, but in view of Mrs Cox's transparent delight at the suggestion all she could do was smile weakly as her eyes spoke volumes.

'That's settled, then.' He turned back to Mrs Cox with a nod of his head. 'And now, if you don't mind, I'll skip that cup of tea. I'm taking Amy out for the day.'

'That's grand.' Blade was obviously the favourite son! 'You two run along and enjoy yourselves.'

She held on to her temper just long enough to reach the car and then exploded with impotent rage as she slid into the lush interior, her jean-clad legs and big baggy jumper incongruous against the expensive décor. She had refuted utterly the idea of changing into more appropriate clothes. These were what she had been going to wear for a day at home with maybe a walk in the hills in the afternoon. If he didn't like it then he could do the other thing, she thought balefully as he slid into the driving seat beside her, looking every inch the wealthy businessman relaxing at the weekend.

Blade didn't seem to object. She was aware of his gaze roaming over the thrust of her high small breasts under the knitted cotton of the pale blue jumper, and became aware in that moment that the V neck was low enough to reveal just a hint of cleavage and that the jeans were just a little on the tight side. She moved her head slightly so that a shining veil of soft gold

hung between them for a brief moment before
rounding on him, her eyes shooting blue sparks.

'What are you trying to do, Blade?' she asked furiously. 'Is this all part of my punishment?'

'I beg your pardon?' He eyed her coolly, eyes
slanted and body relaxed. 'Could you be a little more
specific?'

'You know exactly what I'm talking about,' she
hissed angrily. 'All this friendliness with Mrs Cox and
now offering to do her garden! You're trying to hurt
me, aren't you, discredit me with these people
and——'

'Now just hang on a darn minute.' He caught her
arm so tightly that it felt as though she had caught it
in a vice, and as he shook her slightly, his face was
black with rage. 'I told you before, you have given
up all rights to question my movements in any way.
I'm a free agent now, to do exactly as I please. That's
what you wanted, isn't it?' She opened her mouth to
argue but the logic of his words was indisputable.

'If you feel my presence in this small community
might be a little embarrassing to you and your esteemed "friend", that is nothing to do with me. You
insist, as does he, that you are merely friends. Fine.
Then I see no reason why there should be any talk of
my "discrediting" you. You disagree?' He was
waiting, with a curious watchfulness, for her reaction
and she gulped silently, her head spinning.

'I . . .' She was floundering for words as her heart
thudded wildly. How could she tell him that it wasn't
really the possibility that his presence might em-
barrass her in any way that was worrying her, but that
every minute, every second she was in his company

she was terrified she might give herself away, that he would guess she still loved him. As she hesitated she glanced into his face and the dark, enigmatic expression that had lit the masculine features chilled her blood.

'You are clearly at a loss for words. Well, I can understand that.' There was a hidden threat in the softly drawled words that sent a little shiver trickling down her spine, and as he let go of her arm, settling back into his seat and starting the engine with a turn of the ignition key, his face was closed against her. 'And as to my helping Mrs Cox, the offer was genuine.' He negotiated the powerful car smoothly along the narrow lane. 'I have an excess of spare energy at the moment and I prefer hard work to countless cold showers. Celibacy is not something I'm used to and holds no attraction that I can determine.'

She flushed violently, her stomach tightening as a sudden mental image of the two of them entwined in the throes of lovemaking flashed briefly into her mind. 'You could go back to London, to your job, to—other women if that's what you want.' Her voice was low and painful and she felt him tense like a steel rod at her side before relaxing after a long minute as the breath hissed out of his mouth angrily.

'I'll do you a favour and forget you said that,' he said grimly. 'When I took you into my life and into my bed it was a lifelong commitment, Amy. I, at least, find it difficult to forget that.'

She sank back against the soft leather seat, her eyes bruised and enormous. He was making this so hard, impossible—she'd go mad before it was finished.

'Where are we going?' she asked dully, after a few miles had passed in painful silence.

'I've no idea.' He glanced at her briefly before concentrating on the winding road again. 'I thought we'd drive a while, take in some local colour before stopping at one of your little English pubs for lunch. Sound OK?'

'I don't mind.' Her voice was flat and she heard him draw the breath into his mouth through his teeth in an irritated sigh. Well, she couldn't help it! She was bleeding inside, slowly and fatally. She would never have believed mental anguish like this could be bearable.

The countryside through which they wound was tranquil and sleepy, green hillsides, winding rivers, the inevitable grey stone walls carving an endless pattern up into the rolling summits and down into fields of velvet green grass. Carpets of wild flowers perfumed the clean pure air with their faint scent, spilling over on to the grass verges and down into little dells where sparkling streams sang their way over smooth round pebbles. It was beautiful, magical, but Amy's eyes were blind with misery. I've made such a mess of all this, she thought bleakly as the familiar delicious smell of Blade's aftershave teased her nostrils and tightened her lower stomach into one giant ache. She couldn't see him each day without betraying herself, she just couldn't . . .

'Can you afford to leave the business for days on end like this?' she asked carefully, when they had been driving for some time in cold silence. 'I'd have thought——'

'Consideration? At this late date?' His voice was bitingly cool. 'Don't tell me you are actually thinking of my welfare? Or could it be that you just want to get rid of me as soon as possible?'

'It's just that after our——' She stopped abruptly and as his eyes flashed to her face, their blackness fiery, before returning to the road ahead she knew he had read her mind again and had known what she was going to say.

'After our...?' he asked silkily.

'After our honeymoon you had so many problems to sort out,' she finished in a little desperate rush. How could she have been so stupid as to mention their honeymoon? she asked herself miserably. Talk about a red rag to a bull.

'That's my concern, not yours,' he said shortly, his face dark and cold.

'Blade——' she paused, biting her lower lip help-lessly '—can't we behave like two reasonable people, let the divorce go through as amicably as possible?'

'But I don't feel reasonable, Amy,' he drawled imperturbably, 'in fact I feel anything but. The things I would like to do to you——' He stopped abruptly as his voice tightened and it was a full minute before he spoke again, and then his voice was smooth and controlled with just a hint of cynical mockery. 'Let's just say I don't feel reasonable and leave it at that. Enjoy the drive for now and after lunch we'll have a nice little chat.'

'We've got nothing to say to each other,' she countered quietly as her heart leapt into her throat.

'On the contrary.' He sounded his horn at two large crows who were haggling in the middle of the road over some titbit that looked disgusting. 'There's the tedious business of washing all the dirty linen for a start.'

She sank a little lower into the upholstered seat and shut her eyes tightly for a moment. She was going to have to be careful, so careful. If he even got an inkling of what this was all about . . .

'I understand your white knight, the slayer of dragons, is visiting Mother?' he continued drily with cold mockery. 'I'm surprised he didn't take you along hidden in the boot to keep you from my evil clutches.'

'How do you know John's——?' She stopped as a little bell sounded in her mind. 'Oh, of course, Mrs Cox,' she said flatly. He had really made a killing there, she thought bleakly.

'Has he introduced you to Mummy yet?' the cynical voice continued. 'Or is she one of the old school who would object to her little boy dallying with a married woman?'

'I don't know why you are trying to make John out to be some sort of mother's boy,' she said tightly, 'because he most certainly isn't.'

'Isn't he?' The drawling lazy voice expressed disbelief. 'What exactly are the noble John's attributes, by the way?'

'He's kind and gentle and patient,' she said hotly, as the overt criticism of her friend stung her on the raw. John had shown her nothing but kindness and she wouldn't let Blade, even Blade, make fun of him.

'Worthy virtues in the average cocker spaniel,' Blade said with icy derision, 'but somehow that description is not the most passionate characterisation I've heard in my life. Is that the best you can do for the poor guy?'

'It's impossible to try and talk to you,' she said angrily as the last of her self-control flew out of the window. 'I can't understand why you bothered to come round today——'

'Well, it certainly wasn't to talk,' Blade said softly, without taking his eyes from the road. 'I realised when I saw you again that that wasn't the answer. No, this needs to be sorted out on a more—physical level than just mere words, although they will do afterwards.'

'Afterwards?' she asked icily with all the disdain she could muster through the mad hot pounding of her heart. 'You don't really think——'

'You'd be amazed what I think,' Blade said grimly, 'and none of it good where you are concerned, so why don't you just be quiet now so we can keep things pleasant?'

They lunched at a tiny little wayside inn whose flower-filled country garden sloped right to the edge of a bubbling river banked by smooth round boulders and stones. There were a few tables and chairs dotted about on the rough green grass under the shade of an enormous cherry tree, and Amy voted for a meal in the open when Blade gave her the choice. The quaint little oak-beamed pub with its homely brass and low ceiling was a little too intimate somehow.

'You've lost weight.' They were sitting sipping draught cider in tense silence, the sunlight casting dappled pictures on to the old wooden table through the waving branches overhead, and as Blade spoke Amy jumped involuntarily, spilling a few drops of cold golden liquid as she did so. 'And you're nervy.' He touched her hair, following one silky strand from the crown of her head to its place on her shoulder, his eyes thoughtful. 'Is that because of me, or are you burdened down with guilt at your wayward life?' he asked with caustic mockery.

'According to you I should be, then, I suppose?' she answered quietly as she jerked her head away from his touch. 'You've cast me as the original scarlet woman?'

'You'd disagree with that?' he asked tightly as he settled back into his seat opposite her, his eyes hooded and half closed against the bright light. 'No, don't answer that. I have no wish for you to perjure yourself any more than you have already done. Ah—the food.' For a moment the last three words didn't register, and then a plate of fresh buttered trout, baby new potatoes and fresh green peas appeared over her shoulder.

'Thank you.' She smiled up at the landlady as she spoke, grateful for the diversion. John's words were suddenly very vividly in the forefront of her mind. 'Trouble with a capital T.' And how! She looked at Blade now as he sat eating his lunch with every appearance of enjoyment. The hard, handsome face and big, powerful body were painfully familiar. How many times had she thought she would faint beneath the pleasure that masculine body produced, the intimate sensual caresses that had had her mindless with desire? She turned scarlet at the direction her thoughts had veered off to, snapping her eyes down to her full plate and forcing herself to start eating slowly. She didn't feel like food, she didn't think she would ever feel like food again . . .

She was conscious that the piercing dark eyes were trained on her at regular intervals even without raising her head, and when after a few minutes she pushed her half-eaten meal aside his next words didn't surprise her.

'No appetite? Why?'

'Oh, for goodness' sake!' The vehemence of her voice almost made her jump. 'I'm not hungry, that's all.'

'You don't look as though you have been hungry for weeks,' he murmured wryly, but although the comment might have been airy when spoken by anyone else the hard thread of steel underlying the deep voice told her he wasn't going to let go of this particular bone. 'Or maybe you've been too busy to eat?'

'Blade, you might not have much respect for me now, if any at all, but believe it or not I didn't find it easy to end our marriage,' she said with painful carefulness. 'Obviously it's affected me, it's only to be expected.'

'And that's it?' He leant forward suddenly, trapping her small face between his hands as he forced her head upwards to meet the fiery blackness of his gaze. 'That's all you've got to say to me after what you've done? "I didn't find it easy to end our marriage, obviously it's affected me".' He parroted her words with a furious bitter anger that sliced into her heart.

'Leave me alone!' She tried to jerk away but this time he was prepared and the large hands tightened like iron round her face.

'No way, sweetheart.' Suddenly his American accent was very pronounced. 'Like it or not, you are still

Mrs Forbes for the moment and I'm damned if I'm
going to sit back and do some sort of parody of the
stiff upper lip. What do you think I am——?'

He stopped abruptly as the tears she couldn't hide
any more spilled from her eyes to run a salty trail on
to his fingers. 'Amy!' He swore softly after the one
hard explosion of her name and then she found herself
lifted up into his arms as he moved to her side, his
mouth hard and hot on hers as he strained her to him
in an agony of need he couldn't hide. 'What's got
into you, girl, what in hell's name has got into you?'
His words were a soft groan as his lips left hers and
then she was cradled against his broad chest, the sunlight and everything else fading into a blinding haze
as she sobbed and sobbed and sobbed.

This was the last thing she had wanted to happen,
the very last. Now he'd know she was weak, vulnerable, that there was some mystery. She had to be
strong, had to convince him she knew what she was
doing! But it was useless. She had longed, with a
burning devouring ache night after night, to be held
by him like this. She was deathly afraid of the future,
horribly lonely, but the knowledge that he had ceased
to care, that he believed she had left him because she
no longer loved him, was worse than all the future
might hold. She wanted him to care, wanted him to
share this thing with her, just to *be* there... Sanity
returned in a rush of shame. How could she think like
this? If she really loved him how could she drag him
with her into the pit? None of this was his fault. She
had to see it through alone.

'I'm all right now.' She moved out of his arms
quickly, sitting down in her seat again as she reached

for her handbag and dabbed at her face with a somewhat dog-eared tissue. The effort to control her tears was causing her lower lip to tremble and she bit on it painfully as the coal-black eyes fastened on her face.

'You are far from all right,' he said slowly, 'and I'm fast getting to the point where the temptation to drive somewhere and make love to you until you're pleading and begging me to take you is becoming irresistible.'

The change in conversation threw her and she stared at him vacantly as he took his seat again, draining the last of the cider with a swift swallow. 'What did you say?' she asked faintly as she wondered, for a split-second, if her mind had played tricks on her. 'John——'

'John can go to blazes as far as I'm concerned,' he drawled imperturbably, the poker face he was so good at in business impenetrable and cold. She didn't know why she had mentioned John's name at that precise moment—as a talisman, a protection against the sheer force of sexual energy that was reaching out to her from his big body, she suspected. She found she was shaking slightly, her blood running through her veins at fever pitch.

'I haven't yet worked all this out,' he continued slowly, his eyes never leaving her face for a minute, 'but if you and lover-boy are the epitome of love's young dream, then heaven help the rest of us.' His voice was cool and very remote as though he were exercising an iron control on his emotions. 'So if, as you both claim, you aren't sleeping with him yet, why did you leave me for him? Do you feel sorry for him,

Amy? Is that it? If so, that emotion isn't going to keep you warm in bed when you finally take the plunge, is it? He just isn't your type, face it.'

'Stop it!' She glanced at him angrily. 'Stop talking like this.'

'Why?' He moved closer now, the control slipping as his voice became a snarl. 'Or have I got it wrong, or right as the case may be? Perhaps you are his lover already? Is that it? Does he satisfy you, Amy? Give you what you need——'

Her hand shot out to connect stunningly with his face and as the sound echoed round the empty garden they both froze into icy stillness. 'Well?' One black eyebrow lifted in cool, hard, quizzical admonition but his expression was impossible to gauge as he stood up slowly, his movements faintly reminiscent of a big black cat. 'Is that a yes or a no?'

He was playing with her she thought suddenly as she stared back into the dark, glittering eyes. Taunting her, seeking a weak spot.

'Well, little wife?' His eyes were cold. 'Shall we go for a quiet pleasant walk in this countryside you like so much, somewhere quiet and secluded where we can be alone?'

There was definite cruelty in the lazy, cool jibe, but in spite of the apprehension that clouded her eyes and sent a little shiver of fear snaking down her spine she felt a strange sense of relief too. He didn't suspect the truth or he wouldn't be treating her like this. Those cold black eyes would be soft with pity and the hard face would maybe, however hard he tried to hide it, have a shred of revulsion somewhere in its depths. He

liked beautiful things, beautiful, perfect things, and
she wasn't that any more.

Now she had to be very strong, had to convince
him that he didn't affect her any more, that she meant
every word she had spoken concerning their marriage. Could she do it? She brushed the thought aside
angrily. She *had* to, that was all there was to it.

Once back in the car he drove for just a few miles
before turning off the main road into a narrow earthen
lane banked by high flower-strewn verges and over-
hanging trees. 'Do you know this area?' she asked in
surprise. He seemed almost as though he knew where
he was going.

'I asked in the pub,' he said shortly, 'and they re-
commended this way. We should reach a gated road
in a moment and beyond that moorland.'

True enough, within thirty seconds the gate, gnarled
and old, presented itself and, after they had passed
through, the lane led them up and up until the sweet
wild smell of moorland grass invaded the open
windows of the car and the landscape fell away in
great rolls and curves of patchwork artistry.

Blade brought the car to a halt in a little inden-
tation at the top of a hill, and once the powerful engine
had died the silence, complete and awesome, took over
in all its majesty. 'Come on.' He had left his seat to
move round the car and open her door and now almost
pulled her from the interior, his face expressionless.
'Let's walk.'

She had expected him to begin the interrogation at
once, but instead he seemed wrapped in some dark
silence of his own, walking by her side but careful not
to touch her until they came to a flank in the great

fell where a tiny narrow stream splashed its way over hard grey rock, the water crystal-clear and icy cold. He took her hand to help her across the gully and the contact seemed to trigger his voice. 'Cards on the table, Amy.' His voice was hard and cold and she shivered against its severity. 'It's truth time. And don't forget——' he smiled slowly '—there's just you and me and miles of moorland.'

'Are you threatening me, Blade?' she asked, with far more composure than she felt inside. 'Because if so——'

'If so, I get my hand smacked?' he asked with mocking contempt. 'But don't worry anyway, sweetheart, I'm not threatening to hurt you. Merely——' he paused contemplatively '—merely offering to fulfil my marital obligations.'

And as she took a step backwards, her eyes wide with shock, he laughed very softly and the sound was more chilling than any uncontrolled rage.

CHAPTER FOUR

As she stared at this man she had promised to love, honour and obey for the rest of her life, Amy was vitally conscious of two quite unconnected facts. One was that there was something immensely threatening in the very blankness of the jet-black abyss of his eyes, and the other was a low-moving shadow sweeping across the rolling grassland even as the sunlight followed close on its tracks.

'How long did you think it would be before I found you?' Blade asked softly after a full minute had passed. 'You obviously expected me to try?'

'Not really.' She looked at him warily but the hard face was expressionless now, his eyes veiled. 'I didn't know what you would do.'

'I've checked on the validity of John's injury,' he continued in the same soft voice that was infinitely disturbing. 'And it appears it's genuine.'

'You've done *what*?' She forgot to be cautious as the shrillness of her voice caused the black eyes to narrow into slits. 'How could you? As if anyone would make up a story like that!'

'But it's amazing what people will do, sweetheart.' He eyed her coldly. 'You of all people should know that.' He turned from her, his hard features in profile as he gazed across the grassland. 'I was hoping it was a lie,' he said after a few moments. 'But beating him to a pulp is an indulgence that obviously is denied me. I'll just have to get my satisfaction in another way, won't I?' He didn't look at her as he spoke and in spite of the warm sunlight she shivered helplessly.

'Please don't be like this, Blade——'

He cut off her voice by starting to walk, his back straight and stiff and his body taut. 'Come on, keep moving. I'm less likely to do something I'll regret that way.'

'Blade, please wait.' She couldn't bear this coldness, the veiled threats. This wasn't the Blade she knew. Somehow she had to say something, do something, to defuse his rage. 'I'm sorry...' As she reached his side her voice died at the blackness of his profile.

'Do you know what I've been through imagining you with him, Amy? Do you? *Do you*?' He swung round for one split second and the ferocity in his face brought her heart into her mouth. 'I've been to hell and back a hundred times a day, day in, day out, and all you can say is sorry!' He laughed harshly. 'But those pictures in my mind burnt all the feeling I had for you into ashes...' As his voice cracked, her hand made an involuntary movement towards him but he had turned away again, the big body rigid and stiff. 'I realised after a time that I don't know you, Amy. I never did,' he said coldly after an endless moment when she felt incapable of speech. What was there to say? She couldn't explain, justify her actions. He had a right to hate her after all but, oh, did it have to hurt so much? And it wasn't her fault, she thought painfully, *it wasn't*.

They were following a track at the side of a narrow beck with its own little pools and falls which the gurgling water eagerly explored, and as she stumbled slightly, her foot catching a large tuft of wiry grass, he reached out to steady her, his hand freezing midway as though she were leprous.

'Can I sit down for a minute?' she asked faintly. She couldn't walk and talk like this when her heart was pounding so hard it was making her chest hurt. If only he had left her alone then maybe, somehow, she could have tried to derive some sense of peace from knowing she had done what she had to do. But now? Now she was confused and heart-sore and terribly afraid that she would betray herself. If he touched her . . .

'Sit down there if you like.' He indicated a big smooth boulder at the side of the beck, turning with his back to her as he looked out over the land dipping and rising in front of them. 'How long do you intend to stay here?' he asked grimly, 'in Yorkshire, I mean.'

'I don't know.' She was immensely glad he was calm again, at least on the surface. 'It all depends——'

'On what?' He didn't move but there was something in his voice that made her shiver in the soft sunlight. 'John's progress?'

'I've told you, John is nothing to do with all this,' she said quietly. 'I came here because it was the only place I could think of at the time where I knew someone, a friend.'

'A friend.' The hard voice was inflexible. 'Quite.'

'It's true,' she said flatly, 'I promise.'

His laugh was caustic and harsh and made her jump, violently exploding as it did into the soft warm air with vitriolic savagery. 'You *promise* me?' he said scathingly. 'Well, your track record on promises so far isn't too hot, is it?'

'Look, this is getting us nowhere, Blade,' she said quickly as his eyes raked across her pale face. 'I left because I realised things weren't right, that it wasn't working out. I was trying to be fair to both of us; we were too different . . .' Oh, just listen to yourself, she thought in deep disgust at the banality of the phrases. Is this the best you can do?

'I didn't leave London and some very important business deals to listen to such unmitigated garbage,' he said with dangerous smoothness. 'Things *were* right, it *was* working out and you damn well know it. I left you for forty-eight hours to clinch that French deal and came back to an empty house and the original "dear John". Hell, Amy . . .' His temper was at boiling pitch again and she saw him take a deep hard breath before continuing, his voice several tones lower when he did so. 'You didn't even offer an explanation.'

She stared at him helplessly, opened her mouth to speak and then shut it again with a little snap as her thoughts raced on. She couldn't tell him the truth and her mind refused to come up with a credible lie that would satisfy that sharp mind. Because it was true. They *had* been wildly, exquisitely happy. He knew it and, what was more, he knew she did.

The sunlight had turned his brown hair into the tawny mane of a large predatory lion and she shivered at the analogy as it slipped into her mind. There was no one around for miles—he wouldn't actually hurt her, would he? She stared into the deadly cool eyes lit with a cold fire. She didn't know. She didn't recognise this stranger with Blade's face and body.

'Talk to me, Amy, communicate.' His voice was a biting grate in the warm scented air, a total antithesis to the quiet peaceful scene around them bathed in tranquillity. 'Don't just sit there staring at me with those huge blue eyes as though I'm the devil himself.'

'Whatever I say, it won't make any difference now, will it?' she said slowly as she forced herself to stand upright on legs that felt boneless. 'I want to end our marriage, Blade, I want a divorce, and that's what counts. And you want it now, you told me so. You don't love me any more.'

He stared at her for a long time, something working behind the implacable remote mask that had settled over his face like a dark veil, something that she couldn't read, and then he nodded slowly. 'Yes, I know what I said.' He sighed deeply. 'But it's difficult to believe where we are, what you have brought us to. We had it all, the love, the laughter, the sharing, but for some reason it wasn't enough for you, was it?' It wasn't a question and she didn't try to offer an answer. 'Or maybe it's just that you are shallow, unable to make a commitment that lasts? I've considered that too. I've told myself that you aren't worth a minute more of my time.'

'Then why are you still here?' she asked painfully.

'I'm really not sure.' There was icy contempt in his voice, and as she tried to break the hypnotic power that had her eyes glued to his she found she couldn't. The force of his personality, his iron will, was holding her as securely as any chains. 'Maybe it's as you said? Maybe I want to make you uncomfortable in this quiet little oasis you've made for yourself.' His tone was cruel and mocking as he watched the effect of his words on her face. Words designed to sting and wound. 'Can you give me one good reason why I shouldn't make you suffer?'

'No.' She raised her head proudly. 'Not one.' She flung back her hair as she spoke, unaware of the glorious picture she made standing so straight and slim with her eyes huge in the pale silky smoothness of her skin and her hair a golden mass of light on her shoulders.

Blade's eyes narrowed as he watched her, something dark and fierce springing to life as her gaze didn't falter. 'I thought not.' He let his eyes wander purposefully over her legs outlined under the blue denim, raising his gaze very slowly to her breasts that flowered under his hungry appraisal as though by magic.

She brought her arms round her waist in an instinctive rejection of her body's betrayal, her face scarlet, and heard him laugh deep in his throat, a dark humourless sound. 'You still want me, my deceitful little wife, we both know it.'

'I do not.' She searched for something to say to deflect the situation, which was growing more dangerous by the minute. She needed something to put him off the scent and cut through the cool control; he was lethal when he was thinking calmly. 'You just can't imagine any woman leaving you, can you? The great Blade Forbes, invincible and mighty.' She was being deliberately cruel; it was her only defence and if she didn't use it he was going to make love to her. She could feel it. And then she would be lost. 'You can't accept that I decided I didn't want you any more.'

'No I can't,' he agreed with magnificent arrogance that opened her eyes wide. She had expected him to lose his temper, whip her with words, but there was something thoughtful in the back of his eyes that was more frightening than either of those options. 'And especially not after seeing John. I satisfied you in every way, Amy, mentally, physically. Certainly physically. But there was more to it than that——'

'No.' She had to lie as she had never lied before. 'No, there wasn't. You don't attract me any more——' The last word was cut off with a high squeak of panic as he moved in front of her, his body taut and threateningly masculine.

'I don't?' He eyed her coolly. 'I could have you begging me to take you within five minutes.' The insolent hauteur with which he spoke made her want to hit him even as her mind acknowledged he was absolutely right. She had been so innocent when they married, so naïve, but the sensual world Blade's love had opened up for her had swept away all her inhibitions from the first night. She had been shameless in her desire for him, revelling in the precious intimacy they had shared, secure in his love for her. She had never imagined that a man's body, his lips, his tongue, could fill her with such intense pleasure that the world literally ceased to exist. 'John is too nice, too placid for you, I know it.'

She was unaware that her face had mirrored her thoughts but as Blade reached out to take her in his arms she jerked away as though his touch burnt her, her eyes cloudy with fear. If he made love to her she was lost, hopelessly lost. She musn't let it happen, *she musn't*.

'You are talking about animal desire,' she said sharply as she moved backwards slowly, her face white against the brilliant gold of her hair. 'Lust, physical mating, call it what you like.'

'I *called* it love,' he said furiously, his voice low and bitingly cold. 'I thought you did too.'

'You were my first lover,' she said more quietly, her heart breaking even as she forced herself to go on. She had to finish what she had started; it had to end, *now*. She wouldn't be able to go through this again. 'I had nothing to compare you with, no experience. I realise now——'

'I'm not listening to this.' He cut off her voice more by the look on his face than by his words. 'I'm not sure what's going on, but no one changes this much. You've overplayed your hand, Amy. I don't believe what I'm hearing.'

'That's up to you.' Panic and fear made her voice harsh.

'Exactly.' He had never looked more handsome as he stood there in the warm sunshine, his tanned body hard and strong and his eyes devastatingly compelling as they scanned her face. 'As you said, I was your first lover.' He crossed muscular arms as he continued to stare into the drowning blue of her eyes. 'But, as you know, I had had many liaisons before you. If nothing else they enabled me to recognise the real thing when it came along. And no one acts that good, Amy, not you, not anyone. You loved me, you were crazy about me, nothing you can say could convince me otherwise. I admit when I thought John——' He stopped abruptly. 'But for once in my life I wasn't thinking straight. That's what you did to me, Amy—

broke the tradition of a lifetime.' The self-mockery
was hard and caustic and she hardly dared breathe as
she stared up into his face. One wrong move from her
and they would come together again on this warm
grassy hillside and she would never have the strength
to break free again. She would destroy them both.

'Tell me you don't love me.' His voice was soft now
with a silky sensuality that curled her toes. 'Look me
straight in the face and tell me you don't love me.'

'Blade . . .' She turned away but he moved swiftly,
swinging her round with a sharpness that indicated
he wasn't quite so in control of his feelings as he would
have her believe.

'Tell me.' His eyes were depthless. 'And I'll get out
of your life once and for all. That's a promise.'

His face was so close she could see the thread of
laughter lines leading from his eyes and the odd touch
of silver in the thick virile hair. It brought home to
her how fragile and transient life was. Blade was
thirty-six years old, a strong, virile man in the prime
of life looking forward to having a family with a young
healthy wife. And it couldn't be. Not with her. She
bit her lip hard. This way she was giving him a second
chance. He had nothing if she stayed with him.

'Amy?' He hadn't moved a muscle and even the
air around them was heavy with expectation.

'Blade, I don't . . .' Her voice faltered at the steel in
his eyes but she swallowed tightly as she clenched her
hands into tight fists, her knuckles white. Her whole
body was trembling but maybe he hadn't noticed? She
dropped her eyes from his as she ground out the
words. 'I don't love you.'

'Not good enough,' he said steadily. 'I said you have to look me in the face.'

He had no idea what he was doing to her, she thought desperately. Why had this had to happen to them? It wasn't fair, none of this was fair! She couldn't bear it, she couldn't . . . She raised her eyes and stared blindly into the blur of his face. 'I don't love you.'

The silence was very complete and then, through the pounding in her ears, she heard him breathe out slowly.

'Is that the best you can do?'

It wasn't the response she had expected, and as her vision cleared she saw his face was carefully blank, his eyes hooded and empty. As she stood in front of him, swaying slightly, she felt for a moment he was looking into her soul. 'I don't understand?'

'You and me both.' There was a twist to his mouth that made her want to reach out a hand and smooth the firm lips into a smile.

'I told you.' She lowered her head to stare at a tiny white-petalled daisy lying crushed at her feet. 'You said you would leave if I told you, and I did.'

'You didn't convince me.' She brought her head up sharply to stare into the handsome cold face.

'That wasn't the bargain,' she said hotly, 'whether you believed me or not. You said you would go——'

'So I lied.' His voice was cool and assured and quite unrepentant.

'This isn't fair, Blade——'

'Life's not fair, sweetheart.' Suddenly the chameleon-like skill she had seen him use in difficult situ-

ations in the past was very much in evidence, his whole
manner changing to one of relaxed lazy assurance as
he smiled at her crookedly, his face guileless. 'Now,
as I can see that we aren't going to get any further
this afternoon, I suggest we take a nice leisurely walk
in this beautiful countryside, unless you have a better
suggestion?' The drawling voice and raised eyebrow
was intended to provoke and it did.

'You can go to——'

'Don't tell me where I can go, Amy.' The easy
manner was dropped in an instant, his voice icy. 'You
are treading on a very thin line, my girl, and don't
you forget it. My gut instinct is to take you now and
we both know it wouldn't be rape. However, that
might not be such a good idea as certain parts of my
anatomy are suggesting. It would relieve my frustration which is considerable——' the black eyes
stroked over her hot face '—but I'm not sure at this
moment in time if it would do more. What do you
think?'

'I'll never forgive you if you tried——' She stopped
abruptly as he lifted a hand to her mouth, tracing the
outline of her lips with a thoughtful finger.

'But then as things stand I haven't got anything to
lose, have I?' he asked slowly as though she hadn't
spoken. 'Have I, Amy?' His hand had tangled itself
in the soft silk of her hair at the base of her neck and
as he drew her head back and his own lowered she
felt breathless panic and something else—something
else she dared not dwell on. A fierce hunger and desire
that made her legs fluid.

His mouth was warm and firm and tantalisingly
familiar, and the kiss was long and tender with no

violence or anger in its depths. Part of her knew this was subtle persuasion, she could almost feel the way his mind was working. He intended to prove, to her and to himself, that she was still his. And in spite of everything, in spite of the utter foolishness of responding to him, she was drinking from his lips as though she were dying of thirst. His hands were sensual, intimate—she had no defence against him, no defence at all . . .

'I was mistaken.' As he raised his head and stood back a pace, his voice was dry. 'Five minutes was an exaggeration after all.'

He anticipated her reaction, catching her hand as it moved to strike him, his face sardonic and his eyes watchful. 'Not again,' he said coldly, 'and behave yourself or I'll have to give you another lesson in obedience.'

'Is that what it was?' she asked with painful anger. 'A lesson in obedience?'

'Partly.' He smiled slowly with dark humour. 'But only partly.'

'Then why did you stop?' she asked tensely, as she forced herself to stand straight and still in front of him, drawing her chin up to stare at him proudly with crushed violet eyes.

'Because I don't want mere obedience,' he said softly, 'and you damn well know it. I don't know what you're playing at but you'd better take this on board now and learn it well. I won't be made a fool of, Amy. When we make love again, and we *will*, believe me, it will be because you want it as badly as me but with your head as well as your body. Anything less is second best and I have never accepted that in my life.'

His words hit her like a sword through her heart. Second best? She was that all right. Oh, if only he knew... Her head swam with the intensity of emotion that had drained all colour from her face, and brought the image of the flowers, replaced daily, starkly in front of her. 'No, you never have,' she agreed dully as she brushed a strand of hair absently from her face. 'Why should you? Why should anyone?'

'Amy?' His voice was so fierce it made her jump out of her skin. 'What are you thinking about? John? Has he put that look on your face? Do you have to conjure him up like a weird amulet to protect yourself from the contamination of my presence?'

'Don't be ridiculous.' She forced her face to go blank, removing all emotion from her features which seemed to have the capability to betray her just when she needed to be strong. 'I want to start a new life, Blade, and I want you to do the same. That's all there is to it.'

'I want, I want.' His voice dripped acid. 'There are a darn sight too many "I wants" in your vocabulary, Amy. Well, I have no intention of making this easy for you so chew on that, honey. I can play clean or dirty and I'm damned good at both.'

'I don't doubt it,' she said quietly, as her heart pounded so hard she was sure he could hear it. 'But I shall get my divorce either way.'

'That you will.' There was a hot flicker in the back of his eyes that unnerved her but she took his words at face value and nodded slowly.

'That's all I want.'

'Those two little words again,' he said silkily. 'What a determined little female you are.' She suddenly had the most intense and uncomfortable feeling that through all the talk and overt mockery, that cool and piercingly intelligent mind was ticking away on quite a different sphere altogether. Was she fooling him? She looked deep into the hard face but could read nothing. She wasn't sure any more...

'Can we go back now?' She raised her chin proudly.

'Of course.' He smiled mockingly. 'It would be ungallant to refuse such a beautiful lady anything, especially as she happens to be my wife.' The black eyes were deadly. 'You have nothing more to say to me?'

'No.' She held the lethal gaze bravely.

'Then the choice is yours.' He smiled slowly but the twist to his mouth chilled her blood. 'Lovers not friends. That's how you want it?'

'No!' She glared at him angrily. 'We won't be lovers again, you know that. There's nothing between us, Blade, not any more——'

'Unlike you, I do not go back on my word, Amy,' he said with deliberate laziness. 'I've told you how it will be. You'll want me as much as I want you. You doubt it?'

'I want to go back to the car.'

'So you said.' He made no effort to touch her on the short walk back to the parked car, not even when she stumbled and almost fell. Indeed, he seemed to be almost unaware of her presence as he strolled along at her side, his face cool and closed against her and his powerful body loose-limbed and easy.

She glanced at his face once as he opened the passenger door for her to slide in, but it was distant and withdrawn, a stranger's face in an alien world where there were no colours, just the dank cold grey that

had invaded every pore in her body. The numb misery
that had gripped her mind since that fateful meeting
with Sandra had intensified since she had seen him
again. She wouldn't have thought it was possible but
it had.

But she was fortunate. The little talk she gave herself
periodically had no power even to touch her mind as
she sat silent and small in the powerful car. She *was*
fortunate. She had years left before the disease reared
its head, long years in which to travel, to explore this
beautiful world, to live. What about the children who
were born with crippling disabilities, who never had
the chance to live as she had? She *was* fortunate. She
wanted to press her knuckles against her pounding
forehead but restrained herself. Lots of people were
struck down with no warning; she had been given
time. Precious, precious time. She glanced at the stiff
figure at her side. But she would gladly give up every
second of that precious time just to spend one day
with him as his wife without the knowledge of this
thing hanging over her.

Thank goodness she hadn't conceived his child.
That thought had tormented her for weeks until her
body's cycle had given reassurance. They had seen no
reason to take precautions in the three months in
which they had been married. They both wanted
children, 'at least ten', Blade had informed her
wickedly on their wedding-night after the consum-
mation of their marriage, and with Blade's enormous
wealth the normal financial considerations that
dogged young newlyweds hadn't applied to them. But
the rogue gene that was dormant in boys and attacked

little girls couldn't, *mustn't*, be passed knowingly to another generation.

Life was strange. She bit her lip hard as she thought. In just a few months she had met both ends of the spectrum, Sandra's hate and rage and Blade's love. But now the latter was past tense.

'You'll get cramp.'

'What?' As his deep voice cut into her thoughts she glanced up to find his eyes trained on her for a split-second before he turned to concentrate on the winding country road again.

'Your body is as tense as a rod. Relax.' The tone of voice could have been a weather report for the care or concern it held, but as she looked down at her hands clenched in her lap she realised he was right. Every muscle in her body ached.

He didn't speak again on the drive home through quiet drowsy lanes, cobbled market squares and tiny villages set like jewels in the magnificent countryside. They passed limestone hills, wooded valleys and the odd isolated cottage in pale stone standing serenely at the edge of the road, and still the thick heavy silence that blanketed the car wasn't broken.

As the day began to die, a soft golden twilight lit the great expanse of sky in front of them and as Blade's car drew up outside Mrs Cox's small cottage the melody of evening birdsong filled the air with poignant beauty, bringing a lump to Amy's throat.

'Thank you.' She looked up into his face as he opened the car door for her but it was unreadable, the curt nod he gave her no indication of his feelings at all. And then he was gone.

He reversed the car sharply under the protest of brakes and tyres, speeding down the lane far too fast in a whirl of gleaming metal and roaring engine until both sight and sound faded.

Amy stood for a long, long time in the shadowed lane, moving into the small overgrown front garden after a time to stand with her eyes shut and her back resting against the gnarled trunk of the old lilac tree. It seemed impossible, even now, that this had happened to them, that they were living apart, estranged, with no hope of reconciliation.

Everything had been so right, so good, so many small details adding up to a perfect whole. Blade had understood all her insecurities and fears, his own childhood being one of mixed blessings with devious turns and twists.

His father had married his mother, his second wife, with the responsibility of three children from the previous marriage on his conscience, and his obsessive need still to feature prominently in the boys' lives had cast a shadow over them all.

'We never had a dime to call our own,' Blade had told her quietly, his eyes looking inward and his face cold. 'But my stepbrothers only had to ask and my father would provide whatever they wanted. Todd and I, my brother, grew up accepting that as normal. Mom worked every hour of the day and night to bring some extra money in but there was never enough. They rowed constantly but Mom could never bring herself to leave him like his first wife did. And then Todd died.' His face had been bitter then. 'Meningitis. And my father hardly noticed. It was from that point Mom sort of gave up. For the first time she accepted that he still loved Rosa, his first wife, and that the rest of us were almost incidental compared to Rosa and her boys.' His eyes had been black with pain.

'He was killed in a mining accident when I was eighteen and for years I was rent with guilt that I felt nothing but relief that the rows could stop and Mom could know some peace. She died six years later just as I began to make some real money, when I could have given her the life she deserved. But I've let it go now.' He had held her close. 'I've got you and I can finally let the dead rest in peace.'

And now? She moved restlessly. Sooner or later, perhaps sooner, he would move out of her orbit altogether, living, breathing, sleeping—without her. The shaft of pain through her heart made her gasp in protest. They would be in the same chunk of this little planet but she wouldn't know when he had had a bad day, when he was excited about something, when he was sad. She wouldn't be there to massage the muscles of his neck when he was tense, laugh and tease him about his little idiosyncrasies, lie next to him in the warmth of their huge giant-sized bed... She shook her head helplessly as the tears rained down her face. She loved him, she loved him so much, she couldn't bear this pain... But she had to. She hugged her crossed arms tight into her waist.

None of their dreams could come true any more. He had had such a bad start in life, worked so hard to carve out his success. She would stop him from living the life he loved, fill him with guilt for every time he enjoyed himself without her, and if he did meet someone else...

She sat down on the overgrown grass abruptly, her arms clasped round her knees. And before that time there would be years of waiting, of knowing—a sure-fire time bomb waiting to explode, the knowledge of which would taint even the good days. No children, no young Blade to carry on his father's name. 'I am right.' Her voice was a soft tremble in the cool night air but even as she spoke she raised her head upwards, her wet face shining with ethereal paleness in the dim light. '*I am right.*' This time her voice was firm and harsh, the bleakness that pulled at her delicate features echoed in the three small words that spelt a lifetime of loneliness and solitude.

CHAPTER FIVE

MUCH to her surprise the next morning Amy found she must have fallen asleep as soon as her head touched the pillow. She had expected to lie awake for hours but sheer mental exhaustion had sent her into the transient world of dreams and shadows from which she awoke feeling much much better. Probably the human spirit could only take so much grief in short doses, she thought vaguely as she lay watching the dancing sunlight on the far wall of the small room, but today she felt a sense of peace and surety about her actions that was a balm to her sore heart. She had to be positive, *had* to put the past behind her and forget the future and live only in the present. And she could and would.

That comforting conviction lasted for exactly five minutes, the time it took for her to rouse herself and don her thin silk dressing-gown after brushing her mass of ruffled gold waves into sleek obedience before she wandered downstairs to the tiny kitchen to make herself toast and tea.

'Good morning, Amy.' It wasn't so much the deep rich American voice that caused her heart to stop and then pound madly out of control as the sight of Blade, stripped to the waist and clad only in a pair of grass-stained jeans and light trainers, drinking a cup of coffee with Mrs Cox as he surveyed her standing in the doorway through narrowed black eyes. 'You slept well?' The tone was velvet-smooth.

'What——?' She stopped abruptly. 'I mean . . .'

'I'll just go and hang out that washing,' Mrs Cox said hurriedly, 'now you've cleared all the overgrown grass and moss from the path. Be a real treat, it will, instead of just using that little patch at the end.' She had scuttled out of the back door before Amy could stop her and Blade closed it carefully, levering himself off the far wall where he had been leaning in lazy conversation with the little woman and moving to Amy's side with animal grace.

She tried, with every ounce of will she possessed, to draw her eyes away from that magnificent body but it was no good. The hard, strong male shoulders, broad hair-roughened chest and muscular arms were just as she remembered but better, and as an aching heat spread like wildfire through every vein and muscle she could feel its warmth reflected in her face and, worse, her body. The thin silk of her nightdress and dressing-gown did nothing to hide the hard, pointed tips of her breasts as they responded to the age-old call of his masculinity and she knew, she just knew, he was thoroughly enjoying her predicament.

'I asked you if you slept well,' he drawled mockingly, 'in your chaste little bed.'

'Fine, thank you.' She sidestepped him adroitly and switched the kettle on with shaking hands, knowing full well that in the confined space of the tiny kitchen one wrong movement would bring her up against the tanned hardness of his flesh.

'That's good.' He had moved behind her, his body moulded like a second skin to her back, and as his hands went round her waist and he nuzzled his chin into the scented silk of her hair, she froze helplessly. This felt so good, *so good*... 'You've got your morning smell.' He sniffed into her neck appreciatively and a wave of desire flooded down her spine so hotly she almost fainted. 'A mixture of scented soap, shampoo and something else, something else that is all you. It's——' he growled softly against her skin '—very moreish.'

'You smell of the garden,' she said abruptly as she tried to break away from his grasp. 'And would you please let me go?'

'I didn't smell of the garden when I first got here,' he whispered seductively in her ear, blatantly ignoring the second part of her sentence with arrogant disregard. 'Then I was fresh and cool from my shower and with a little of that aftershave you like so much. Remember?'

Did she remember? Her senses were racing in hyperdrive as she caught the sensual, heady scent of the exclusive aftershave he had made specially for him, a mixture of lemon, musk and something altogether wicked.

'I didn't sleep too well,' he continued lazily as he settled her more firmly into the hard planes and contours of his body, his warm breath causing a million ripples of sensation she fought with all her might to hide. 'In fact after three cold showers at two, four and six respectively I thought maybe a spell in Mrs Cox's garden would get rid of some of my excess energy. It was working too, until you walked in half naked.'

'I am *not* half naked,' she protested vigorously, turning angrily in his hold as she did so. It was a mistake. Now she was facing him and the slight slackening of his arms that had enabled her to shift her position tightened instantly as the soft curves of her body were pressed against the length of his. 'Let me go, Blade, I mean it. I——'

The pressure of his lips on hers caught the words in her throat and his mouth was immediately possessive, the kiss a deliberate, experienced assault on her senses. She was painfully conscious of her breasts caught against his hard hair-roughened chest, the thin layer of silk separating them more erotic than any nakedness, and as his tongue sent a river of desire coursing through her body she felt her mouth become pliant and eager beneath his.

'Mrs Cox...' she muttered desperately, her head spinning.

He growled, deep in his throat, at the protestation. 'Would be only too pleased to see a husband kissing his wife good morning.' He had raised his head just long enough to speak and she saw his eyes were hot and glittering, their black depths brilliant. 'Now be quiet and let me finish the greeting.'

She tried, momentarily, to stop him but then his hands and lips were caressing her again and she sank dizzily into the sensual warmth, her senses whirling. He was just too good at this, he always had been.

'Now, then.' As he raised his head a minute or two later Amy knew it had been just in time. Another few seconds and her legs would have given way completely. 'Tell me you didn't enjoy that.' His gaze stroked mockingly over the taut outline of her breasts displayed in evocative detail under the clinging silk.

'I didn't want you to kiss me.' She stared at him, her face scarlet. 'I've told you——'

'That you don't love me. Yes, I know.' His eyes were hard now, hard and cool. 'But that isn't what I said. Tell me you didn't enjoy it.' He moved back a pace, crossing powerful arms over his bare chest. 'And that will confirm you've turned into a duplicitous little liar, my love. Because that was your body giving the go signals there, and if it weren't for the fact that our esteemed Mrs Cox might be a little put out to find us *in flagrante delicto* on her kitchen floor I would be very tempted to give you exactly what you were asking for.'

'You arrogant, overbearing...supercilious...' Her rage was making her flounder for appropriate descriptive words, especially in view of the laconic relaxed mockery evident in every line of his face and body.

'I plead guilty to the first two, but the third...' He eyed her tauntingly. 'No, not the third. I know the things I'm good at, Amy, and making love is one of them, it's as simple as that. If you don't like it, then tough.' Suddenly the lazy mockery was infinitely more chilling. 'And when I'm ready I will have you and you won't be able to do a thing about it. And do you know why?' She stared at him without speaking, her blood running cold at the biting contempt and anger in his face. 'Because you'll want it as badly as me if not more.'

'Never.' Low as her voice was, it caused his face to darken into lines of pure steel.

'I've never accepted that word from anyone in my life and I sure as hell don't intend to start with you.' He gave her one last scathing look that caused her flesh to burn from the top of her head to the soles of her feet before stalking out into the garden angrily, his head held high and his back straight.

She watched him, her nerves shot to pieces, as he exchanged some passing comment with Mrs Cox, who was still hanging her washing out in the fresh summer air, before he picked up the old garden spade and began digging in one of the overgrown flower beds. The sunlight turned his bare torso into rippling bronze as he applied himself to the task in hand, and as she stared it came to her, on a flood of something approaching hysteria, that no one in the world would believe that the big muscled giant working in the garden of a little Yorkshire landlady was the multimillionaire Blade Forbes who had the business world at his beck and call. She didn't know whether to laugh or cry so she did neither, turning to automatic as she made herself tea and toast and escaping to her room before Mrs Cox came back into the house.

'I hate him.' She found she was talking to herself as she paced the bedroom agitatedly. 'He's doing this on purpose, working here on purpose.' She stopped for a moment and pressed close fists against her temples. 'Why is he doing this, why can't he let go?' The answer was there the instant her mind voiced the question. Because nothing and no one had ever got away from him before; she doubted if anyone had ever wanted to try, anyway. She had seen at first hand the effect he had on women. 'Lethal,' she muttered to herself irritably. And he had told her he didn't want

her back, that he didn't love her any more, but . . .
She opened her eyes to gaze unseeingly across the
small room. He needed to know he could still have
her physically if he wanted to. Was that all their marriage had meant to him in the final analysis? Was it?
She rubbed her hand over her eyes wearily. No, she
didn't believe that, but just what she did believe she
wasn't sure any more. He was different, very different, but then he could say exactly the same about
her.

One thing she *was* sure about was the necessity to
avoid being alone with him at all costs. She stopped
to stare into the mirror on the old wardrobe door
blankly, her eyes skimming with perfunctory interest
over the delicate beauty that had first attracted Blade.
For most of her life her beauty had been a lead weight
round her neck, alienating Sandra, destroying any
closeness she might have had with her dour aunt and
uncle, and now proving an ongoing temptation to
Blade even when he despised her and a snare to herself
because it kept him near.

But he had loved *her*. Not just her looks. She turned
from the mirror with a little cry of despair. Hadn't
he?

By the time she was ready for work she was cool and
composed, her hair secured in a tight knot on top of
her head and her body clothed in a loose flowing skirt
and baggy top that hid her figure almost completely.
She examined her face devoid of even a trace of make-
up anxiously. She looked quite ordinary like this, she
did. No one would look at her twice. If she had voiced
that thought to anyone else they would have stared at

her as though she were mad, their eyes appreciating the silky honey-gold smoothness of her flawless skin, the wide, heavily lashed violet eyes and thick rich mass of golden hair whose beauty couldn't be hidden even by the tight severe hairstyle, all the things Amy had ignored. Indeed, the strict lack of adornment and chaste hiding of her body under the somewhat voluminous clothes were a subtle temptation in themselves if only she had known, accentuating her natural attributes rather than concealing them.

She took a deep breath as she left the sanctuary of her room, vitally aware of Blade in the small front garden below. He had worked in the larger back garden for most of the morning and she had heard his voice laughing with Mrs Cox in the kitchen at lunchtime, although she had remained firmly and determinedly in her room. Now he had moved round to the front garden which meant she would have to see him again as she left. Had he done that on purpose? She gritted her teeth as she opened the creaking front door quickly. Probably...

'I'm just going to pop into the next town for some grass seed,' he said in reply to her hasty goodbye as she passed him almost at a run. 'You're obviously late; would you like a lift?'

'I'm not late.' She resigned herself to looking at him and turned round carefully, little tremors of sensation curling her nerves as she watched him reach out to a nearby branch and unhook his shirt from its natural wooden hanger. 'I'm meeting John at the end of the lane, actually; he sometimes gives me a lift to work,' she finished weakly as the dark eyebrows rose mockingly with scornful amusement. 'It's kind of him.'

'Oh, definitely.' He eased his body slowly into the shirt without taking his eyes off her. 'Very kind.' She felt her stomach constrict as his muscles rippled and relaxed. He *had* been waiting for her, quietly, like a big powerful animal that waited patiently for its prey and then pounced without a shred of pity or compassion to deflect its aim. This devious sexual baiting was deliberate; he knew exactly the effect his body was having on hers, and what was more was making the most of every minute.

She stared at him for a long moment without replying, but the hard sardonic face didn't waver in its dark amusement at her discomfiture, the black eyes merciless. 'I don't like this side of you,' she said slowly as she turned away from him, 'it's cheap and——'

'Cheap!' His eyes weren't amused any longer; instead they were filled with a blazing anger that made her realise she had gone too far. 'You talk to me about cheap!' He had swung her round with such force as he spoke that she had landed with a hard jolt against the rigid wall of his chest, and now he held her forearms with both hands, his face as black as thunder. 'You're asking me for a lesson in manners, my girl, and this is one time——'

'Amy!' Mrs Cox's voice from just inside the house caused him to stiffen momentarily, his hands as hard as iron, before the bruising grip loosened as he moved her away from him with a little exclamation of disgust.

'What the hell am I bothering for?' he said slowly, his eyes dark with contempt. 'Go and keep your date.'

'Amy?' As Mrs Cox appeared in the doorway to
the house the landlady's round face broke into a
pleased smile. 'Oh, I'm glad I caught you before you
left, lass. Arthur phoned. He's had to go out himself
to pick up some meat that should have been delivered
earlier and he said to be sure and take your keys so
you can let yourself in. Have you got them?'

'Yes, Mrs Cox.' The normal tone of voice and small
smile that she stitched on to her face took more effort
than Mrs Cox would ever know. 'Thanks. I'll see you
later.'

She turned and was out of the gate before another
word could be spoken, her head high and her back
straight, although the hot tears coursing down her face
made the narrow lane in front of her a green haze.
He had looked at her as though he hated her then,
really hated her. But that was what she wanted, wasn't
it? she asked herself bitterly as she walked swiftly
away. No, a small still voice deep in her head answered
quickly and painfully. She didn't want that at all.

'Stay away from me, Blade.' She spoke out loud
into the still warm air as she walked quickly down the
lane shaded by huge old trees on either side. 'I can
take the pain and the loneliness and everything else
if you'll just stay away.' But he couldn't hear her in
the final analysis and she wasn't sure if she wanted
him to.

John was waiting in his usual spot parked to one
side of the lane in a gated pull-in that overlooked
roaming fields full of grazing sheep. 'Amy?' His
smile had faded immediately he had seen her face.
'What's wrong?'

'It's Blade.' She took the handkerchief he offered as she sank down into the worn seat next to his and sniffed dismally. 'He's helping Mrs Cox with the garden.'

'He's doing what?' John stared at her in blank amazement. 'I don't believe it.'

'Neither did I at first,' she said quietly. 'And he's so hostile——'

'He's hurt you?' John glared back down the lane angrily.

'No, nothing like that.' She took another deep breath and managed a wan smile. 'I'm just being silly. He'll give up and leave eventually, he'll have to. I'll just have to manage till then.'

'This is crazy.' John slipped his arm round her shoulders and gave her a comforting hug. 'Do you want me to have a word with him?'

'No.' She shook her head slowly. 'That would be the worst thing you could do. He's got this idea that we're—you know.' She paused in embarrassment. 'I'm sorry, John.'

'Don't be.' He smiled down at her, his mild blue eyes warm. 'It's an enormous compliment to me. You've never thought about me like that, have you?'

'Of course not.' She smiled again. 'We're friends, aren't we?'

He was very still for a moment before sighing gently as he moved her round to face him. 'Friends?' He nodded slowly. 'That definitely, but I would like there to be more. You must know how I feel about you, Amy? How I've always felt? You were so young when we first met, I didn't like to push things and of course I was tied up with Carol then, so the whole thing was

impossible. But when I got the wedding invitation...'
For a moment the face looking at her was quite unlike
John's. The placid easy expression had gone and in
its place she read—something she didn't want to read.

'John, please——'

'No, listen to me, Amy.' He was still holding her
tight and she felt unable to move away. 'I shall regret
it for the rest of my life if I don't tell you how I feel.
When you came here, to me, I couldn't believe it at
first. It was a dream come true. Oh, I know you look
on me as a friend.' He shook her very gently as she
opened her mouth to speak. 'You've never given me
any reason to hope for more, but now?' He moved
fractionally closer. 'You've left Blade, Amy, for
whatever reason, but the fact remains that you've left
him. Do you think you could learn to love me, learn
to care?' As he moved to take her mouth she turned
her head abruptly and his lips merely brushed her
cheek, but in the same instant she heard, rather than
saw, Blade's car flash past them on the dusty road.

'John...' She took a deep breath as she struggled
away and he let her go easily, looking out of the
window at the cloud of dust left by Blade's powerful
car, as his brow wrinkled in consternation.

'Was that...?' he asked slowly.

She nodded miserably. 'He was going to get some
grass seed,' she said weakly. 'For the garden,' she
added unnecessarily. Her mind buzzed frantically, less
with the content of John's declaration than the fact
that Blade might have seen them as he shot by and
assume—what would he assume? The worst, no
doubt.

'Well, I'm sorry, but it doesn't alter anything——'

She cut off John's voice with a little shake of her head, her eyes pleading for his understanding as she looked into his round familiar face. 'John, I'm sorry...' She paused, unsure of how much to say. She hadn't wanted to tell anyone about the illness but perhaps——

'There is no hope?' He looked at her for a long moment before nodding his head slowly. 'I think I knew really, but I had to say it. You forgive me?'

'Don't be silly, there's nothing to forgive.' She touched his arm gently, moving her hand away as his face tightened. 'It's just that I love Blade, John, I have from the moment I met him and I always will. I value you as a friend, my best friend, and if things had been different—but they're not.' She didn't want to say too much, but if John thought Blade was in some way responsible for her leaving she owed it to him to explain a little.

'It wasn't Blade's fault I left but I can't explain beyond saying you'll have to trust me in this. He didn't do anything wrong, just the opposite.'

'Then why——?'

'Please, John.' She shook her head slowly as her face whitened. 'I can't explain. If I could talk about this with anyone it would be you, I promise, but I can't. Not yet anyway.'

'Amy, if you're in some kind of trouble?' He stopped abruptly. 'I'll do anything, anything to help, and forget all that I just said. There'd be no strings attached.'

'Oh, John...' She was fighting to keep back the tears, desperately touched by the emotion he had revealed and his staunch friendship when he must be hurting too, feeling about her as he did. She should never have come here, upset his life, but she hadn't known. She had thought he was fond of her on a purely platonic footing; he had never *said*, never indicated in the tiniest way in the past that he felt anything more than benevolent detached affection. 'John, I'm so sorry.'

'No problem.' He moved firmly away and settled back in his seat, his face suddenly resigned. 'But I'm here, always, if you want me. Understand?' He glanced at her from the corner of his eye. 'And I meant what I said, no strings attached. Now, let's get you to work before Arthur starts hollering.'

The afternoon and evening were long and difficult, with a host of minor irritations that had her wanting to scream by the time she was due to leave. The little restaurant was hot and sticky, and owing to the non-delivery Arthur had been forced to fetch they were working behind schedule most of the day. And she felt so bad about John. And Blade. And everything...

Suddenly all the doubts and fears that she was doing the right thing returned in a devastatingly bitter flood. She wanted Blade, needed him; she couldn't handle this any more.

She had a sudden fierce desire to be utterly selfish, to tell him the truth and lay the burden on his broad shoulders and let him deal with it as he would. But almost as soon as it was born the notion died. What would it accomplish? At the best he would view her with a mixture of love, pity, compassion and maybe, threaded through all the other emotions, revulsion. At the worst she would destroy his life from the moment she admitted the truth.

She loaded the dishwasher in the small kitchen, with her jaws clenched so hard it made her teeth ache. This self-pity had to stop. She had made her bed, now she had to lie on it, *alone*.

'Amy?' The night was warm and mild, a bonus from the unusually hot day, and as she stood for a moment on the step of the restaurant sniffing the clean air filled with a hundred summer scents she felt a sharp stab of pleasure that *now*, at this instant, she was still vitally and strongly alive. The future was wrapped in shadows and a long way off. 'Now' was this quiet balmy evening in a little Yorkshire village with the sweet tang of woodsmoke hanging on the still air and the fragrance of green grass and wild flowers drifting in from the moorland and hills beyond.

Blade had carried her off to the Caribbean on her honeymoon, with brief stops in the South of France and Switzerland, but nowhere in the midst of all that spectacular beauty had such intense pleasure and sadness combined to make one moment so piercingly sweet.

'Amy?' As Blade spoke her name again it penetrated the trance, bringing her back to reality with painful suddenness. 'I want a word with you. I'll give you a lift home.'

He moved out of the shadows to stand looking up at her and she noticed the car, parked some yards away, for the first time. 'A lift?' She stared at him almost stupidly as her senses registered that he looked all male and incredibly dangerous in the black cotton trousers and shirt he wore so easily. 'I think not. And we have nothing at all to talk about, Blade. It's over.'

'I'm not disputing that,' he answered coldly, something gleaming in the dark depths of his eyes she couldn't quite fathom. 'But as we both seem to be living in the same small village for the moment we need to get the ground rules sorted, and they don't include necking with lover-boy in full daylight.'

'But you don't *have* to live here,' she answered hotly, suddenly furious at his manipulation of events.

'And you do?' He eyed her arrogantly. 'Well, do you?'

'Yes,' she snapped tightly, 'and if you were half as sensitive as I thought you were you'd just leave me alone. I don't need——'

'But I'm not sensitive, Amy, am I?' he drawled slowly but with an iciness that was chilling. 'And no doubt there are many other things in which I'm lacking too. But as for what you need or don't need——' the black eyes were like stone '—I really don't give a damn.'

'Then why are you here tonight?' she asked desperately. 'What's the point in torturing me like this?'

'Oh, come, come.' He sounded almost bored. 'A little dramatic, don't you think? And I've told you why I'm here.'

'I was talking to John, just *talking*,' she said to his cold face. 'You're trying to drive me away from here, aren't you?' she stated with flat painfulness. 'This is part of my punishment, this hounding?'

'If it were, why should you expect anything different from me?' he asked coldly. 'I haven't exactly noticed any love and consideration in your dealings with me lately, or maybe there's something I've missed?' The sarcasm was scathing. 'You can't have it all ways, Amy, or haven't you woken up to that little fact of life yet?'

She stared at him helplessly without replying, but there must have been something in her eyes that revealed her anguish, because in the next instant he was at her side, his face black with a mixture of rage, confusion and something else, something banked and hidden behind the jet black of his eyes. 'Damn you, Amy. I should walk away from here and cut my losses...' He took her arm, forcing her down the steps and towards his car with such speed that she felt her feet weren't touching the ground. 'If you let him touch you again——'

'Let go of me!' She tried to pull away but only succeeded in jarring her arm so hard it made her eyes water. 'Blade!' There was real panic in her voice and as they reached the car he opened the door and pushed her inside in one movement.

'Stop screeching,' he said coldly, as he slid into the driving seat a second later as she sat rubbing her arm helplessly. 'I have accepted your opinion of me is pretty low, but even I draw the line at abduction if that's what you are worrying about. I'll drop you home later but first I tell you the ground rules regarding lover-boy. OK?'

'No, it's not OK,' she said furiously as the colour came and went in her face in rapid succession. 'And how dare you manhandle me like that? I'm not some stray parcel that you can throw about——'

'No, you're my wife,' he said with bitter rawness, his eyes flashing. 'And I for one take that seriously. I thought at first that you'd looked on this as a game, our marriage, everything. But now, now I'm not so

sure. Having seen you with John . . .' The penetrating
gaze swept over her white face and now that piercing
discernment that made him such a formidable adversary was in full force. 'I think there's something
more, something I can't quite get yet. You were everything I wanted in a woman, Amy, everything I'd
dreamed of, and for a time I lost sight of the fact that
I'm an excellent judge of my fellow man.' The arrogance was hot and fierce. 'I still do when you make
me angry.' His face was reflective as he turned to look
out of the windscreen into the darkness beyond. 'You
are the only person who can make me lose control
like that.' It wasn't a compliment and she kept quite
still, hardly daring to breathe.

'But, when I'm thinking logically, I know I couldn't
have been fooled so completely. So——' he looked at
her again, his face proud and imperious '—I have to
assume that something happened in those forty-eight
hours when I was in France. Something momentous.
It could be another man other than John, but my enquiries haven't revealed anything to substantiate that.
I know you left very early that first morning in the
car and returned late at night from the servants but
other than that——' he eyed her coldly '—nothing. I
don't like mysteries, Amy,' he continued expressionlessly, 'I never have, and this one least of all.'

'I want a divorce.' He was getting too close. 'That's
all that matters——'

'No, my beautiful little wife, that is *not* all that
matters,' he interrupted harshly. 'I have to accept now
that you can be selfish and cruel, the facts speak for
themselves, but one thing I know for sure is that you
aren't happy. You might have done something that is

eating you up with guilt, whatever—I don't know. But
I will.' She couldn't bear the derision in his eyes. 'Because I want my pound of flesh, Amy. Now that's not
nice and it sure isn't the British way, but I'm not
British.' He laughed caustically. 'And your body still
holds a certain appeal.' He laughed again and the
sound chilled her blood. 'As mine does for you. Don't
bother to deny it; that gets boring after a time.'

He started the engine as he spoke and the big car
growled immediately into life, the bonnet nosing into
the road as the powerful headlights lit up the darkness.

'Are you trying to make me hate you?' Her voice
was a whisper in the shadowed confines of the car.
'Is that the plan?'

'Hell no,' he drawled mockingly. 'It'd perhaps be
fun but—no. I've just decided to take a short va-
cation, sweetheart, soak up a little history, and a spot
of hill walking while I'm here, and where better to
relax than this place that you seem to love so much?
Tell me, Amy.' His voice had altered now, its coolness
wry and hard. 'Do you ever lie awake at night thinking
of me with an ache in your body that won't go away?
Thinking of the things we used to do? How you used
to groan my name over and over again—— '

'Stop it,' she said tensely. 'I won't listen to this.'

'Won't?' he challenged laconically. 'A little strong,
surely, when you are in my car being driven at fifty
miles an hour with the door locked? I wouldn't have
thought "won't" came into it.'

For a moment Amy felt pure rage drive every other
emotion from her body. He was being cruel, hateful,
and she didn't know how to stop it. It was as though
he had given himself over to some hard force that had

sucked all his finer feelings into an empty void so that all that remained was his darker side.

'Well?' He raised black eyebrows in mocking invitation. 'Not lost for words, surely? Tell me again that I mean nothing to you, that it was all a mistake, that your body isn't crying out for mine this very moment. Tell me, Amy. I missed out on fairy-tales when I was younger; I'm about due for some now.'

'I hate you.' It was true, she did. Didn't he know this was all for him, that she was suffering tenfold anything he was enduring? He could never have loved her, *really* loved her, to treat her like this now.

'I'll buy that,' he said grimly. 'I'd have preferred something a little less caustic but at least hate is real, more real than this rubbish you've been handing out to me for days. You can't ignore hate, Amy, it won't let you.'

'I haven't ignored you.' She stared at him in amazement. 'I've never ignored you.'

'Then you're one hell of an actress, sweetheart,' he said harshly. 'Once or twice back there I began to think I was the invisible man; out of sight, out of mind. But I won't stay out of sight, will I? That's what really rankles, isn't it? Did you really think I wouldn't want more than a few words scribbled on a piece of paper? That you could just glide out of my life like one of your English milkmen delivering a daily pinta? ''Sorry, the cream's off from now on, skimmed will have to do?'' Well, I want the cream, Amy, and I'll have it one way or the other.'

'You're talking about sex,' she said flatly.

'Am I?' He was driving far too fast for the narrow winding road, but she didn't care. Right at this moment in time she didn't care about anything. 'Well, if you say so it must be true. You've got everything sewn up, after all; who am I to argue? But I tell you one thing, if I see that slime-ball touch you again there'll be murder done, crutches or no crutches.'

She thought it prudent to ignore the insult to John for the moment as she glanced at his stony profile, black with rage, and concentrated on the first part of his statement. 'You *are* talking about sex,' she said quietly. 'Animal lust! And where are we going, anyway? This isn't the way home.'

'To take your first point, if you remember I did give you the option and you chose not to compromise. Lovers not friends, remember? As to the second, you are quite right, this is not the route to Mrs Cox's safe little house.' His voice was sardonic and cold. 'This leads somewhere quite different.'

'Where?'

He didn't miss the note of alarm in her voice and smiled in mocking satisfaction. 'Have patience, sweetheart, all will be revealed,' he said smoothly, all emotion carefully banked now. 'You can't come to any harm, after all; we are married, remember—it's quite legal.'

'If you are planning rape, that isn't legal in any situation, married or not,' she said tightly as she forced back the tell-tale tremble of fear from her voice. 'I'd never forgive you——'

'Rape?' He actually had the effrontery to smile, and but for the fact that, as he had pointed out before, they were travelling at breakneck speed on the curving country road she would have hit him hard. 'Within a few seconds of my touching you it won't be rape,

Amy, and we both know that. But you are assuming rather a lot, aren't you? As far as I'm aware, you haven't even been asked.'

She drew her hand across her eyes distractedly as she fought for composure and the strength to control the trembling that was threatening to take over her mind as well as her body. Part of her couldn't believe that they were talking like this.

'I thought perhaps the noble John would be waiting in his chariot?' Blade drawled after a long moment with cynical mockery. 'Especially after the touching scene at lunchtime.'

'He's gone to London for his treatment,' she said stonily as she kept her gaze straight ahead. 'And I told you, we were just talking.'

'You *tell* me a lot of things, sweetheart,' Blade said with dangerous smoothness. 'It's picking the wheat from the chaff that proves troublesome.'

'I'm not arguing with you, Blade——'

'That will make a pleasant change,' he said drily. 'Well, just sit back and enjoy the ride.'

'Enjoy the ride'. The phrase brought Sandra in front of her as vividly as if her sister were in the car.

She had been surprised, surprised and relieved when she had arrived at her sister's house that morning and been granted access. On the long journey down she had anticipated a harsh rejection like before when she was just sixteen and desperately eager to renew her acquaintance with this, the last of her flesh and blood. But this time Sandra had allowed her to enter the house, and as her husband had shown Amy into the large downstairs room that Sandra occupied as a bed-sitting room, he had tried to prepare her for the change she would see.

'She's ill, Amy,' he had whispered quietly before knocking on the old paint-chipped door, 'but it's a good sign that she's agreed to see you. She needs to make her peace with you, come to terms with the past.'

'I don't understand.' Amy had looked at his kindly face, her blue eyes wide and puzzled. 'What do you mean?'

'Sandra will explain.' He had knocked then and pushed her into the room quickly. 'I'll be out in the garden if you need me. I'll come back later with some coffee.'

Her sister had looked up as she had entered and Amy had flinched inwardly at the change in her. Six years had wrought havoc. 'Amy. Dear, sweet, gentle little Amy.' Sandra's voice had been low and tight and Amy had paused in her headlong flight to her side. 'So you've come back at last. I was hoping you would.'

'Were you?' Amy stood uncertainly in the middle of the shabby room looking down into the bitterly twisted face.

'And your husband?' Sandra's eyes had narrowed. 'He's not with you?'

'No.' Amy had a strange feeling as the hairs on the back of her neck stood on end. There was something evil in this room, something cold and infinitely depraved, and she found herself wishing with all her heart she had stayed at home. 'He's away on business.'

'Of course, the high-flyer.' Sandra laughed softly. 'He would be.'

'Yes, well...' Amy forced herself to look into the dark gleaming eyes. 'How are you?'

'How am I?' Sandra's body had been twisted slightly in the wheelchair, a large car rug covering her lower half and her hands resting on the arms of the chair. 'I'm dying, Amy, didn't you know?'

'You're...' Amy's voice had choked away and she took a deep breath before continuing. 'Your husband said you were ill, but I didn't understand——'

'There are lots of things you didn't understand when you came in here, but you will before you leave.' There had been immense satisfaction in Sandra's throbbing voice, satisfaction and malignant gratification. 'But here's me forgetting my manners. How are you, little sister?' And Amy had known, at that moment, that something horrendous was going to take place. 'Are you enjoying the ride?'

'The ride?' Amy tried to smile but found it was beyond her.

'The ride of life,' Sandra had hissed malevolently. 'There you are with your wealth and looks and rich, rich husband. You must be enjoying the ride—you are, aren't you?'

'I—yes, I am, yes.' She was having a job to speak coherently; there was something in this room that was freezing the words in her throat.

'Good.' Sandra had smiled with diabolical ferocity. 'Well, I have some news for you, little sister.' And then it had started, the destruction of her world...

'Here we are.' As Blade's voice brought her back to the present, she gazed in alarm at the small cottage in front of them set in its own neat garden without another dwelling in sight. 'This is the cottage I'm renting, quiet, secluded——'

'And lonely.' She glanced round at the wooded countryside on all sides. 'Where's the nearest house?'

'Half a mile away.' He smiled slowly. 'Peaceful, isn't it? There's a small stream that runs through the bottom of the garden and a den of badgers in that copse beyond, but it's still only five minutes to the village.'

'I'd have never put you down as a country bumpkin,' she said coldly as he moved round the car to open her door. 'And there is no way I'm getting out of this car, Blade. I want to go back, *now*.'

'Country bumpkin?' He leant for a moment on the open door, apparently considering her words. 'Well, if by that you mean I like it here, then guilty as charged.' He eyed her piercingly. 'But I also like the bright lights, don't get me wrong. I am a man of big appetites, Amy, and I am in the fortunate position to be able to indulge them.' The innuendo was clear and she flushed angrily, dropping her eyes from his.

'I meant it, I'm not getting out of this car.'

'Don't be tiresome,' he drawled lazily. 'I'm offering you a cup of coffee at the end of a long day and a look round this place, that's all. At the very least you should come in and phone Mrs Cox to explain where you are and that you'll be a little late.' When she still didn't move his tone became more caustic. 'Amy, I'm a grown man of thirty-six and well past the stage of groping at every opportunity. I want to get our relationship on a more civilised plane, that's all. Now be a sensible girl and get out of the car before I have to lift you out. You are the one who doesn't want any physical contact, after all.' He laughed softly and her nerves twanged at the derisive amusement in both his voice and face.

'Have I a guarantee that you'll remember that?' she asked tightly, 'if I come in for a while?'

'Of course.' A wicked grin that caught her heart like an iron fist lit up his dark face briefly. 'As long as *I* can be sure that you will treat me accordingly. I've had the nasty notion more than once recently that you've got designs on my body...' His rich chuckle at her furious face was just the spur she needed to get out of the car, refusing the hand he held out to her with cool disregard. He thought he was irresistible, did he? His ego really was jumbo-size.

'Now then.' As he opened the old wooden front door and ushered her through into the beautiful little room beyond, his voice was quietly satisfied. 'Come into my parlour, said the spider to the fly.'

She glanced at his hard handsome face for just one second as her blood ran cold. This was a trap, a carefully stage-managed trap, and suddenly she knew just how that fly from the old nursery rhyme had felt. But it was too late now, much much too late.

CHAPTER SIX

'Do stop looking so tragic.' They were seated in front
of the carefully restored old fireplace which domi-
nated the small room, which was all old wooden
beams and traditional cottage fare, the pretty chintz
covers that covered the two large winged armchairs
matching the curtains at the narrow leaded windows.
'I'm not going to eat you alive.'

She raised her eyes from the fireplace slowly. The
first thing that had registered on her after her initial
panic had been the enormous bunch of fresh flowers
in place of a fire, the beautiful display that scented
the air with summer chilling her very soul. She
couldn't have had more apt confirmation that what
she was doing was right, she thought bitterly. 'Do you
replace these daily?'

'What?' His eyes were puzzled.

'The flowers.' She took a sip of the scalding hot
coffee he had just brought through from the quaint
little kitchen, hoping it would calm her racing nerves.
'Do you get fresh ones each day?'

He glanced from her pale face to the delicate blooms
and then back again, his gaze narrowing at the expression in her eyes. 'No.' He leant forward slightly
as he spoke, searching her face intently. 'They're from
the garden outside. It's a mass of colour in the daylight but it would be a shame to rob it of all its beauty.
Those are a few days old, but I change the water daily.'

He was speaking mechanically as though his mind were elsewhere. 'Why did you ask that, Amy? It seemed as though it was important to you in some way.'

'Of course it's not.' She tried to smile but it was a dismal failure. 'I just wondered, that's all.'

'I see.' It was obvious he didn't but she was relieved he had decided not to pursue the matter. 'Well, what do you think of this place? Cute, eh?'

'It's very nice,' she responded carefully.

'You should have come upstairs.' His voice was bland but his eyes were wicked as he noted the pink in her cheeks. 'The two bedrooms are real old world England, sloping ceilings and tiny diamond-leaded windows——'

'I've been in plenty of cottages in my time, Blade,' she interrupted stiffly. 'I do know what they look like upstairs.' She took another desperate gulp of coffee and glanced at her watch for the fifth time in as many minutes. 'I really ought to go now.'

'Would you like a brandy with that?' he asked lazily as he gestured towards her coffee, completely ignoring the content of her words. 'You look as if you need one.' He appeared overpoweringly masculine in the small pretty room, the black shirt and trousers emphasising the lean hard power of his big body and the tanned darkness of his skin. He stood up slowly as she shook her head, his eyes thoughtful. 'That must be painful.'

'What?' She stared up at him in confusion as he stood over her, the deliciously clean smell of him causing her stomach muscles to clench in protest.

'The way your hair is strained back. Your scalp must be screaming in protest.' He reached out a large hand and released the knot in one deft movement, standing back in approval as her hair cascaded on to her shoulders in a riot of rich gold. 'Now tell me that isn't better.'

'It was fine the way it was,' she snapped quickly. 'And I must go now, Blade, please.' She fumbled with her hair helplessly, her cheeks flaming with colour. This could all easily get out of hand, which was probably exactly what he had planned. Why, oh, why had she been so foolish as to get in the car in the first place? And she must have been mad to follow him in here. What would the psychiatrists say about that? she thought bitterly; that she secretly wanted him to sweep away all her objections, overpower her with his superior strength?

'In a while.' He sauntered across to a small occasional table standing underneath one of the windows and poured her a small measure of brandy, blatantly ignoring her earlier refusal. Another delaying tactic?

'I said no.' She eyed the dark alcohol in the bottom of the balloon glass warily. 'Aren't you having one?'

'I don't drink and drive,' he said shortly. Once seated again he stretched out his long legs comfortably, his body relaxed.

Unlike hers, Amy thought painfully. Every nerve-ending was throbbing with awareness, her whole nervous system as tight as a coiled spring. He, on the other hand, seemed almost unaware of her presence and as she peered surreptitiously under her eyelashes she saw to her chagrin that his eyes were closed and his head laid back.

'What are you so frightened of, Amy?' He didn't open his eyes as he spoke and the deep voice was almost expressionless.

'I don't know what you mean,' she said flatly as her heart pounded.

'I think you do.' He adjusted his position in the chair and smiled a cold hard smile, still without opening his eyes. 'A cat on a hot tin roof would be easy to have around compared to you. What is it you're hiding?' Now the black eyes opened and their intensity was unnerving. 'A one-night stand? Something like that?' His very stillness was intimidating and she took a deep, long breath as she met the piercing eyes.

'Is that what you think?' she asked painfully.

'The ball's back in my court again?' He eyed her laconically. 'Very clever, sweet thing. No, as it happens, I don't think that, not now, but where you are concerned I've discovered I can't quite trust my feelings as I can in every other area of my life. I don't like that, Amy.'

'I'm sorry.' She stared at him, nonplussed by the cool control.

'I want you, physically, very much.' His voice was almost conversational. 'In spite of everything that's happened that doesn't seem to fade. Damn inconvenient really.' He sat up in one fluid movement and now she saw the real Blade for one piercing moment as his eyes met hers before the shutter came down and masked his soul from her gaze. There had been a fire blazing away there, an angry, vitriolic fire that wanted to consume and destroy, and for the first time since entering the cottage she felt pure undiluted fear flood through every limb and tissue.

'Yes . . .' She stood up slowly, frightened to move too quickly, to do anything that might set loose the monster behind the man. 'Well, if you're ready . . .'

'I'm not.' He eyed her grimly. 'And you haven't touched your brandy.' She watched him silently as he reached for his cup, swallowing the contents in one gulp. 'More coffee?'

'No, thank you.' She sank back down on the seat as he strode out into the kitchen, perching on the very edge of it with her hands bunched in her lap and her knees tightly together as she heard him pour himself more coffee.

'Your solicitor has informed mine that you want no financial settlement of any kind. Is that true?' His voice spoke from the kitchen, harsh and abrasive, and she winced inwardly at the tone.

'Yes.' Her voice died in her throat and she tried again. 'Yes, that's true. This is all my fault after all, it wouldn't be fair——'

'What, exactly, *is* all your fault, Amy?' He appeared in the doorway and her heart nearly stopped at the sight of him. He was so cold, so angry . . . If she could stop loving him, wanting him, needing him, this would be so much easier, but she knew with dreadful finality that no matter what he said or did to her it wouldn't make any difference. He was everything she had always wanted, dreamed of, in the long cold years of growing up without love and warmth. And now he despised and hated her. And it had to stay that way. 'I mean, I'd really like to know, strange as it may seen, in spite of being an almost irrelevant complication in your life. I wouldn't expect a little thing like a husband to stop you following your own star but, if it's not too much trouble, a slight indication of why would be helpful.'

She stared at him, her eyes wide with apprehension and confusion, as he came nearer. What could she say after all? 'I *have* told you,' she forced out at last through white lips as he paused to kneel at her side, his eyes narrowed black slits. 'I just realised we'd made a mistake, that's all, that we weren't compatible——'

'*The hell we aren't.*' She had known, from the first moment in the cottage, that he was going to make love to her and now as the heat of his mouth seared her lips open she found her resistance was only a token gesture. Her head knew she ought to fight him, that she had to prove to him that she meant what she said, but her body was a different matter. That was alive with such a fierce deep hunger that even a will of iron would have melted with the heat. 'You are mine, Amy, you'll always be mine. If I really believed you'd slept with John, I'd kill him...'

How they came to be on the thick sheepskin rug in front of the fireplace she wasn't quite sure, but as she felt the length of his body against hers all lucid thought was a thing of the past. Her hands lifted to his shoulders and the back of his head, her fingers luxuriating in the feel of his thick virile hair as she brought his head down to meet her lips. His mouth was intoxicating, sensual, and now his hands slid from her waist to open her blouse feverishly, seeking and finding the firm silky line of her breasts as he expertly unclipped her bra and let the burgeoning swell free.

His touch was like fire on her overheated senses, the rolling waves of pleasure that swept her body unmistakable, and as his mouth followed his hands in a seductive caress that had her aching for more, she whispered his name over and over again, half mad with desire.

Her fingers were stroking the hard male body under his shirt, revelling in the familiar feel and smell of him, and as he raised his head again to find first her mouth and then the shell-like sensitivity of her ears she felt the need inside her grow to unbearable proportions. It had been so long. She had been in the desert place so long.

'I need you, Amy.' His voice was thick and deep, an echo of her own heart, and now the tide was carrying them both to the ultimate conclusion, fierce and unstoppable. 'You are so perfect my love, so very perfect.' *So very perfect*? His words were bitter gall in her mouth.

For a moment he didn't realise she had frozen beneath him, his desire a fierce consuming fire, but then as she wrenched her mouth from his and beat her fists frantically against his back she heard him groan deep and harsh in his throat. 'Amy, you can't do this . . .'

But even as he spoke he rolled away, sitting up in one violent movement as his breath filled the small room in shuddering gasps.

He had stopped. She lay exactly as he had left her, her clothes dishevelled and open, her heart pounding so sickeningly that for a moment the room faded away. He could have taken her, he had been so close, but in spite of all his threats and accusations he had stopped.

They remained in a frozen tableau for a full minute as he fought for control, and then he stood up slowly without glancing at her once. 'I'll be outside when you're ready,' he said expressionlessly, his voice empty and cold. 'Take as long as you need, you have all the time in the world.'

She heard the front door open and close and then she was alone, surprised to find that she was crying soundlessly, her tears soaking her hair into wet tendrils that clung stickily to her face. He would never forgive her for this, she thought bleakly into the deathly silence as she sat up slowly, adjusting her clothing with limp shaking hands. She had made things so much worse, or maybe...? She closed her eyes as a thought pierced her heart—maybe they had had to get this bad for him to finally accept it was over? But she didn't want it to be over. The words were fierce and hot in her head. She wanted him to keep trying, wanted him close because if he went away... Her eyes opened very wide. He would never come back.

She stood up wearily, her head pounding. She was going mad, insane... Of course it had to be over, she knew that. What was the matter with her? 'You're cracking up, girl,' she whispered to herself flatly as she combed the wet tendrils of her hair back from her face slowly. 'You are so perfect, so very perfect'. The cataclysmic blow he would never understand, but which summed up everything. She wasn't perfect any more, she was badly flawed and beyond repair. 'A beautiful little doll.' Sandra's words were engraved on her soul in letters of fire, but her eyes were dry by the time she joined him in the car. He glanced once at her white face and then concentrated on the darkness beyond the headlights. 'Do I take it that was an object lesson in how adeptly you can switch on and off?' he asked harshly, after a few minutes had screamed by in absolute silence.

'I didn't plan it, Blade,' she protested quietly without looking at his dark profile, wincing as he made a deep sound of disbelief in his throat. 'I didn't!' she said more vehemently. 'Can you say the same? That you didn't have this evening all worked out?'

'If I did it sure wasn't one of my best deals, was it?' he growled bitterly and with scathing cynicism. 'I thought I *knew* you, Amy, I mean really knew you. I would have trusted my life on that belief. Hell!' He shook his head angrily as his face hardened into cold steel. 'I hate a bad loser.' She missed the self-contempt in his voice, hearing only the words themselves.

'A bad loser?' She turned to stare at him in the darkness. 'Is that all our lovemaking meant to you, one of us winning while the other lost?'

He stiffened, his knuckles white on the steering-wheel, before relaxing slowly after long seconds as he let his breath out between his teeth in a cool tight angry sigh. 'That's about what you would expect from me, isn't it?' he answered coldly. 'You've made that perfectly clear. And maybe you're right. According to you there was only ever physical love between us, sex in its crudest form, anyway? At least on your side. Right?'

She froze, unable to reply. '*Right*?' The word was a pistol shot in the darkness.

'Yes!' She took a deep breath as she forced herself to go on, to put the last nail in her coffin. 'I realise that now. As I said, you were my first lover and I mistook what I felt, our physical attraction, for love. I had nothing to compare it with, no way of knowing...' Her voice trailed away at the complete stillness of his body.

'I don't believe you, Amy,' he said at last, his voice calm now. 'I'm darned if I know why, but I don't. Call it intuition or sixth sense or whatever, but there is more, much more, to all this. But I can see that for whatever reason you have made up your mind, and I won't try to dissuade you any more. Our marriage is over. I accept it.'

'You do?' Where was the relief? The conviction that she had done the right thing now, when she needed it most?

'Yes, I do.'

The rest of the drive home was conducted in tense silence but never had she been so aware of the big male body next to her. Every movement, however slight, brought her over-stretched nerves to breaking point, and as they drew into the lane leading to Mrs Cox's cottage she turned to look at him, her face white.

'This is goodbye, then,' she stated expressionlessly. 'I suppose you'll go back to London tomorrow, you must have a lot to do.'

'Yes, I have a lot to do.' As the car drew to a halt he left the engine running as he came to open her door. 'But I've made a promise to Mrs Cox so I shall be around for a while yet. You needn't worry——' his voice was mockingly derisive '—I'll leave you alone.'

'Thank you.' If the world had stopped, thrown off its axis at that precise moment, she wouldn't have cared. It was all too much. He was going to go, in a day, a week, believing that it was what she wanted. She shut her eyes tightly for a second. *She* had to accept it was over. She never had before, she thought wonderingly. Why hadn't she realised she had been holding on? 'Goodbye, Blade.'

She passed him without looking up into his face, walking with careful measured steps to Mrs Cox's front door and slipping inside quietly like a small ethereal shadow. As the door closed behind her, Blade remained staring at it for a long, long time, and when, eventually, he sat back in the car his face was wet and his fists tightly clenched as he drove them against the hard unyielding dashboard time and time again.

CHAPTER SEVEN

IF ANYONE had told Amy that she would laugh again, especially in Blade's presence, she wouldn't have believed them, but that was exactly what she found herself doing five days after the fateful visit to Blade's cottage.

The intervening days had settled themselves into a pattern almost without her being aware of it. Blade arrived mid-morning to work in the overgrown jungle of a back garden, where he remained until after she had left for work. From the vastly improved appearance of the front garden she assumed he moved there once she was safely out of the way to avoid any chance of their meeting. It hurt, but not as much as seeing him would, she reminded herself grimly night after long night when she lay awake tossing and turning into the early hours.

If she thought about it, it frightened her that she barely recognised herself any more. The old Amy had been very young and childish, painfully insecure and with a need to be loved that had been almost obsessive. The new creature born of all the anguish and hurt was different... She didn't know if this new woman was better, she only knew she was different.

John had said much the same thing when he had called in the restaurant the day before for a late lunch. She found that she was suffering more for Blade than herself, which gave her the courage to go on. He, at

131

least, would have the chance of a long and full life
once he had put the bitterness concerning their marriage behind him, but it was the final irony that the
new Amy would have been a tower of strength to him
if things had been different, she thought painfully.
When she thought back, in the peace and quiet of the
long night hours, there had been so many times when
he had arrived home tired and drained with the de-
mands that his huge empire made on him. He drove
himself too hard. She nodded to herself in the shadowed darkness. But the chance to tell him was lost
now.

She had just returned to her room on the morning
of the fifth day with a cup of coffee and some toast,
made hastily before Blade arrived, when she heard his
deep rich voice with its American accent greet Mrs
Cox in the kitchen. Her heart thudded into her mouth,
but she was getting used to that now, she reminded
herself firmly, and then for a few minutes all was
silence and tranquillity.

The uproar, when it happened, was sudden and intense and at the same moment as she became aware
of Blade swearing loudly and profusely, Amy heard
Mrs Cox calling her name frantically. She took the
stairs two at a time, thankful she had dressed early
in jeans and T-shirt, to enter the kitchen in a burst
of adrenalin that stopped abruptly at the sight that
met her eyes.

'It was a swarm of bees,' Mrs Cox gabbled quickly.
'He must have disturbed them.'

'A swarm of bees?' She repeated the little woman's
words vacantly as she gazed at Blade, big and heart-
stoppingly attractive, but undeniably rattled as he

glared at Mrs Cox ferociously, his bare torso and legs pinpricked with red.

'There was no need to cause such a fuss,' he ground out irritably through clenched teeth as he raked back his hair harshly. 'A few bee stings never hurt anyone.'

'Unless you're allergic.' Mrs Cox was determined to make a drama out of a crisis. 'My sister's boy nearly died with just one. Terrible time of it he had. Swelled up like a balloon.'

'Thank you, Mrs Cox.' Blade's face was a study in self control. 'But I shall be perfectly all right, I do assure you.'

'I think we've got some cream somewhere.' Whether it was hysteria born of anti-climax or the sight of Blade totally out of his depth for once Amy didn't know, but the desire to laugh was growing dangerously by the second. He was so furious at being caught out, so enraged that the small insects had had the temerity to attack him, that she had to bite her lower lip until it drew blood in an effort to keep control, and Mrs Cox didn't help, continuing to describe her nephew's brush with death at the hands of a bee with enormous relish that increased at Blade's lack of a suitably awed response.

'Here we are.' As Amy fished the tube of cream and antihistamine pills out of the first aid kit in the back of the big pantry, she motioned for Blade to sit down on the kitchen stool. 'I'll just bathe the stings with cold water first and make sure none is left in,' she said quietly, 'before I put the cream on.'

'I'm perfectly able to do all that myself,' Blade replied stiffly, very much on his dignity, the effect of which was spoilt slightly by the carefulness with which he sat down on the stool and the red patches burning on his tanned skin.

'Where's the swarm now?' Amy asked blandly, after she had ascertained all the stings were out and had daubed cream over the marks on his back, Blade insisting that he do the rest himself. She didn't protest; there had been something immensely sexy about his vulnerability that had her hands shaking before she had finished applying the cream to the big, hard-planed body.

'You'll have to excuse me, but I didn't stop to find out where they went,' Blade said scathingly as he moved to the kitchen window and peered out. 'I was rather preoccupied myself.'

'Ran in here like a greyhound,' Mrs Cox supplied helpfully, 'swearing like a trooper he was. Banged the door shut so hard it's a wonder it didn't fly off its hinges.'

It was the final straw. The picture that Mrs Cox had conjured up was so unlike the smooth powerful businessman and ruthless tycoon that the world knew that Amy felt the last of her composure melt on a flood of laughter that was unstoppable. She was aware of Blade's face changing from one of aggrieved surprise to wry humour and then he was laughing too, his eyes rueful.

Quite when her laughter changed to tears she wasn't sure, but at the same time as Blade lifted her up into his arms as he sat back on the stool she was aware of Mrs Cox quietly slipping away into the small front room closing the door gently behind her. 'I'm sorry...' She tried to pull away but the hard masculine arms tightened as he pulled her closer into his hair-roughened chest, and then the flood-gates really opened, the tide unstoppable.

It was a good few minutes later before the racking sobs turned into tearful hiccups and then stopped altogether, but as they died she became aware that Blade's arms were wonderfully comforting, his strength non-threatening. 'Better?' He raised her tear-drenched face by lifting her chin carefully, gazing into the drowned violet eyes searchingly.

'I'm sorry,' she said again, her cheeks scarlet as she tried to move out of his arms. 'I didn't mean——'

He sensed her panic, his voice soothing. 'Relax, sweetheart, relax. I haven't taken this little display of normal human weakness as an invitation in any form. This is just a friend comforting a friend, OK?'

'You said we weren't friends any more,' she said shakily as she slid to her feet, her hair tangled gold, its colour all the more vivid against her white strained face. 'Remember?'

'In certain circumstances we have to adjust,' he said with dry humour, his eyes warm. 'Once you are your old self again we can resume hostilities, if you insist.'

'I don't want us to be enemies, Blade,' she whispered honestly, her eyes enormous. 'I want...' Her voice trailed away.

'I don't think you know what you *do* want,' he said slowly. 'You sure are one mixed-up lady.' Again he sensed her withdrawal at the oblique probing and he finished the moment of intimacy by getting to his feet and reaching for the small tube of ointment. 'Are you going to continue the Florence Nightingale act?' he asked drily. 'Because one of those little hornets made a short and fatal journey into the inside of my shorts,

the result of which needs attention. Care to inves-
tigate?' His eyes were wicked and she blushed hotly
as he lowered his denim shorts in careless disregard
of his nakedness. 'You could always kiss it better,' he
suggested, his face straight, as he daubed a small blob
of cream strategically in place before hoisting the
shorts into place again and swallowing a couple of
the small white tablets.

'I've got to get ready for work,' she said faintly,
escaping out of the kitchen to the sound of a deep
mocking chuckle of dark amusement.

Once back in her room she paced restlessly, her head
spinning. That was stupid, *stupid*, she told herself
frantically as she relived the scene below. He'll
think... What would he think? She shut her eyes
tightly as she sank down on the small narrow bed.
She didn't know. She had never understood that cool
analytical mind that was so dangerously astute and
intelligent. She knew he was feared, as well as highly
respected, amongst his peers with a reputation for
striking straight at the jugular with deadly precision,
but with her he had been different. From carefully
stage-dropped remarks at parties and such like she had
gathered he could be just as ruthless in his private life
as in business and yet with her... She shook her head
slowly. He had been gentle and tender and wonderfully loving.

She expected him to be waiting in the front garden
for her when she left an hour later and had nerved
herself for the inevitable confrontation, but as she
stepped out of the small front door only green veg-
etation and gently waving trees greeted her troubled
eyes. It was a beautiful day. She glanced up into the

pure blue sky, washed clean of even the faintest trace of a cloud, as the breeze lifted her hair into a silky cloud round her cheeks, feeling the sun warm on her upturned face. Some wallflowers, their velvet petals bright and glowing, wafted their heady perfume into the thick warm air and a group of tiny sparrows flew by in a noisy game of tag. *She was alive*. She shut her eyes with the intensity of the thought. And for years yet she would be able to walk and talk and see normally, travel, explore the far corners of the world before it was too late.

But she couldn't have Blade. Suddenly all the rest seemed infinitely pointless, a dark grey cloud descending with abrupt coldness over the colour and warmth of the day before she forced the depression away with rock-like determination. After the first week, when she had wallowed in stunned shock and morbid self-pity, she had made a vow to herself as she clawed up through the blackness that had enveloped her since Sandra's venom had poisoned the very air she breathed. No more indulgent self-pity, no more crying for the moon and no more tears. Well, the last part had been impossible to keep but the rest was up to her.

'You're no wimp,' she told herself out loud as she walked quickly down the lane, the gently rustling branches overhead an arched canopy of green, 'and you're not going to waste an hour, a minute of precious time with pathetic whinging. OK?' She continued, in fits and starts, to lecture herself all the way to the small restaurant and amazingly, by the time she served her first customer, the world was in place once more. And Blade was still around for the moment.

She nodded to herself slowly. How she would cope once he left, really left, she didn't know, but for the present he was here. She could hear his voice, catch a glimpse of him now and again and that had to be enough.

The unusually warm weather for late May brought a host of tourists into the restaurant and the small dining-room was still packed at closing time. It was well after twelve before the last customer left and Amy was free to leave, and the effort to put one foot in front of the other was fast becoming impossible. The emotion of the morning coupled with sheer hard work had drained all her natural resources and she found herself dreading the short walk home. It was with a mixture of emotions then that she saw Blade's car parked directly outside as she stepped out into the dark sleepy street.

'Amy?' His voice was soft and deep as he called through the open window before sliding out and coming to meet her. 'You look all-in.' As she looked at him it came to her, in a flood of self-awareness, that she had been desperately hoping he might meet her and the knowledge made her voice unnecessarily sharp as she stared up into his waiting face, his solid strength and male bulk poignantly attractive.

'I thought we'd agreed you would leave me alone,' she said tightly, dropping her eyes from his as she moved to turn away. 'I don't want you to meet me, Blade, you——'

'Just a minute.' All the tenderness had vanished and his voice was now as cold as ice. 'I have something to tell you——'

'I don't want to hear it.' She didn't know why she was behaving so badly, but found it impossible to stop. 'How many times——'

'Will you shut up, woman!' He was shouting and he never shouted, she thought with a small detached part of her brain that seemed to be looking on as an interested spectator. 'Give me strength . . .' He raked back his shock of hair angrily and took a deep breath before he spoke again. 'It's Mrs Cox.'

'Mrs Cox?' she repeated vacantly. 'I don't understand?'

'Apparently her sister has been taken ill; a neighbour phoned this afternoon. Bronchitis that turned into pneumonia and now there are further complications. She's in a bad way, I understand.'

'Oh, no.' She stared at him helplessly. 'But her sister's all the family she's got.' Mrs Cox's husband had died in the war before they had had any children, and she had preferred to live as a widow in the tiny village in which she had been born rather than join her sister and her elderly husband in Scotland. Since the death of her sister's husband a few months before the two had become even closer, exchanging letters and phone calls nearly every day.

'She left on the afternoon train,' Blade continued more quietly, 'and I promised her I'd keep an eye on the house—and you,' he finished grimly. 'Now get in the car and stop behaving like a bad actress in a third-rate movie.'

'Well, how was I to know?' she protested weakly as she slid into the luxurious interior that smelt of leather and subtly expensive aftershave. 'I thought after this morning——' She stopped abruptly and turned to meet his eyes that had turned stony.

'You thought after this morning I would press my supposed advantage?' he finished tightly. 'Charming, really charming, Amy. What I ever did to deserve you I'll never know.'

They were home in three minutes, and as Blade drew up outside Mrs Cox's cottage he was out of the car before she had even loosened her seatbelt. 'Go in and check everything's all right. I'll wait here,' he said with bitter cool contempt. 'I'll be round as normal in the morning, so if you want to do the princess-in-an-ivory-tower act you'd better get your breakfast early. Mrs Cox gave me a key, incidentally, so there's no need to leave doors open.'

'Right.' She opened her mouth to say more and then shut it as the full force of his glittering gaze swept over her face. Now was not the time to apologise. That much she *could* see.

She could feel his eyes burning into her back as she walked to the front door, and after switching on the lights and making sure everything was as it should be she raised her hand once to him as he sat glowering in the car, whereupon he screeched off immediately in a cloud of dust and burning tyres.

'Oh, damn...' She sat down weakly on the hall chair as her legs began to tremble with a mixture of exhaustion and reaction. 'Damn, damn, damn...'

The next morning she packed herself a picnic brunch and left the house very early, her eyes red-rimmed with lack of sleep. She had to be at the restaurant at just after one as usual but the walk she had planned should bring her within yards of the doorstep, and she needed to get away into the swelling countryside beyond the village where the air was heavy with the sweetness of fresh green grass and heather in full bloom.

She ate her meal in the shade of an enormous oak tree surrounded by the smell of thyme and wild garlic, leaning back against the huge old trunk as she watched the silvery flowing river in front of her cascading over great rocky shelves and massive slabs of stone.

She ached for Blade, longed for him, with a fierce primitive desire that had no reason or logic in its fire. She wanted to live with him, share those odd private moments with him, have his babies ... The thought brought her bolt upright from the dreamy trance she had slipped into as she watched the flowing water in its timeless motion.

Have his babies? For a second she actually put her hand to her heart at the intense physical pain that had shot through her. Children? She stood up quickly, brushing the last of the crumbs from her skirt with a shaking hand.

She would never feel new life growing and moving inside her, know the joy of seeing a tiny little screwed-up face bellowing for milk and then settling with rapt enjoyment at her breast as a hungry little mouth sucked its fill, never know——

'Stop it!' The sound of her voice echoed out over the water like a lost soul.

'There'll be no morning sickness, no stretch marks, no waddling.' She gazed up into the green branches overhead, the leaves a thick blanket that filtered the sunlight with complete effectiveness. 'And no growing old, no arthritis, no grey hair.'

What was she doing? She gazed round her suddenly. Talking to herself as though she were crazy! This solitude wasn't such a good idea after all. It gave her too much time to think.

Work provided its normal therapy but she found herself peering out of the door as eleven came and went, half hoping and half fearing to see Blade's car in the street outside. But it was empty.

When she left, fifteen minutes later, she didn't notice a tall dark figure detach itself from the shadows and silently follow her at a discreet distance, remaining carefully in the background until she had reached the safety of the cottage and the lights were burning to announce it was occupied. Blade stood outside for some time in the velvet darkness, his face unreadable and his hands thrust deep into his jeans pockets before turning in one savage movement and striding back the way he had come.

And within a few minutes the lights in the cottage went out.

Although Amy had been conscious of Blade about the place—the continuing improvement to the garden, a stock of his favourite beer in Mrs Cox's small fridge—she hadn't actually met him face to face since the evening Mrs Cox had left. He had resumed the routine of working in the large back garden until she left at lunchtime and she had been equally careful to stay out of his way, so when she awoke on the following Sunday morning to the delicious smell of roast beef permeating the small cottage she assumed Mrs Cox had returned during the night and hurried downstairs without even bothering to pull a robe over her thin silk nightie.

'Good morning.' Blade turned from his task of preparing fresh vegetables at the kitchen sink, his eyes narrowing at her scanty attire, and raised one large hand in mocking salute. 'And mine has improved considerably in the last ten seconds.'

'I thought you were Mrs Cox.' The heat that began in her face rapidly covered her whole body as she stood transfixed in the doorway. What *did* she look like? Whatever it was, Blade obviously approved if the wicked light in his eyes was anything to go by. 'And you shouldn't be here.'

'Says who?' He leant back against the sink, letting his eyes run over her from head to toe with slow thoroughness before turning back to his self-imposed task with a lazy shrug of his big shoulders. 'There's a bottle of wine in the fridge if you want to open it.'

'Me?' Her voice was an outraged squeak of protest. 'Like this?'

'I'm not complaining.' There was a throb in the deep voice that told her he was finding this present situation highly amusing. 'But I can wait a few minutes if you want to change into something—less comfortable? But, please.' He turned again and this time the look in his eyes made her whole body tingle with sensual awareness. 'Not on my account.'

'But you shouldn't even be here. What if Mrs Cox——'

'Amy.' Her name was a cool rebuke. 'Go and get changed, sweetheart, before my more basic instincts take over. It's been three months, and the sight of you like that is more than I can take right now.'

'And three weeks and two days.' She didn't know why she said it, but he became very still as she spoke. 'I do *know*, Blade.'

'Sure you do.' He moved across to her, looking down into her face for a long moment before turning her gently round and pushing her towards the steep narrow stairs. 'And for the record Mrs Cox knows I'm here. I've phoned her a couple of times to see how her sister was and so on.'

'Have you?' She turned at the top of the stairs, unaware that the shaft of sunlight streaming in through the high narrow window made the silk transparent. 'And how is she?'

'As comfortable as can be expected in the circumstances,' he said drily, 'which is more than can be said for me, incidentally. For crying out loud go and get something on that beautiful body before I come up there with you.'

'I'm going.' She sped into the bedroom with her heart thudding and her knees weak. Why had he come? *Why* had he come? She had been doing so well. Admittedly she couldn't eat or sleep but that would get better in time. And the tears were always a blink away, but that was only to be expected. All things considered she had been doing well, she *had*.

She dressed carefully for optimum neutrality in a big baggy T-shirt that came to just above her knees and cotton leggings in jade-green, brushing her hair vigorously before tying it into a high ponytail on the top of her head. Make-up? No. She shook her head at herself in the mirror. No make-up. No come-on. *Definitely* no come-on. It appeared he was cooking lunch. Fine. She would eat it politely, make some small

talk and then indicate it was time for him to leave.
No problem.

Her thoughts mocked her as she entered the kitchen
again to find the back door open on to the garden,
the scent of dog roses and wall-flowers competing with
roast beef. 'I'm out here.' Blade's voice called to her
lazily. 'Come and see the transformation and offer
suitable homage.'

It was true. The back garden had been transformed
in just over a week from an overgrown, if colourful,
jungle into a delightful cottage garden in which mature
cherry, apple and plum trees competed with flowering
bushes and neat flowerbeds hosting a mass of perfumed blooms round a central lawn that was neatly
mown. 'The lawn's still a bit patchy, but the grass
seed will see to that in time,' Blade said laconically
as she didn't speak. The sight of him stretched out
on a long low sunbed almost naked had temporarily
robbed her of coherent thought. 'Come and have a
glass of wine, it's all ready. The sunbeds are a little
gift to Mrs Cox, by the way.' He eyed her lazily. 'I
thought we might as well use them today with the
weather so hot.'

'Fine.' She perched on the edge of hers as though
she were afraid it was going to bite her, accepting the
glass of wine Blade offered with a stiff little nod of
thanks. He was clad only in brief bathing trunks, his
muscular tanned body stretched out to the golden rays
of the sun with supreme disregard for her blood
pressure.

'Look's like we're gonna have a blazing June,' Blade
drawled slowly after a few tense moments had crept
by in absolute silence. 'Wouldn't you be more

comfortable in a bikini or something? It must be seventy-five degrees out here.'

'No thank you, I'm fine.' Oh, listen to me, she thought desperately. What did fine mean?

'Fine?' It was as though he had picked up her waveband. 'You don't look fine, Amy.' He sat up suddenly, the rippling of hard compact muscles and firm flesh causing her ears to sing as the blood pounded madly through every vein. 'You've lost even more weight.' It was a very definite admonition and she flushed angrily as she lowered her eyes to the wine glass in her hand, taking a long sip of the glowing liquid that tasted of mellow, ripe fruit and warm golden days. 'And you seem quite exhausted.'

'We're busy at the restaurant,' she said quickly, her voice defensive, 'what do you expect?'

'I expect you to relax when you get the chance,' he answered mildly, even as the searching intensity of his glance belied the soft tone. 'Now we are two grown adults, Amy, not a couple of nervous fourteen-year-old virgins trying to resist the urge to experiment. Go and change and have an hour's therapy in the sun before lunch.'

'But you just told me to *get* dressed,' she argued aggressively, her eyes angry. 'Didn't you?'

'Well, now I'm telling you to get *un*dressed.' He studied her for a moment as she still didn't move. 'It's an order, not a suggestion, Amy, and for crying out loud don't turn everything into a major confrontation.'

'I don't!' She met his gaze head on, her eyes hurt.

'You damn well do.' He lay back on the lounger again, his big powerful frame stretching like a sleek

dangerous animal relaxing before the kill. 'I'm not
going to jump on you if you display a little of that
gorgeous body, if that's what's worrying you.' His
voice was insultingly light and the derisive laughter
that followed brought her head snapping upwards and
her body tensing in protest. 'You may imagine you
are irresistible, but I assure you you'll be perfectly
safe.'

'Too true I will,' Amy snapped back violently
through gritted teeth. 'I shall make sure of that.'

'Well, there's no problem then, is there?' he drawled
with unforgivable amusement at the easy way he had
provoked her into doing exactly what he wanted.
'You've made it quite clear, by word of mouth and
actions, that you no longer find my ardour welcome.
So be it.' He took a long sip of wine before lying back
and shutting his eyes against the mid-day glare. 'I'm
devastated of course,' he continued with dry sarcasm,
'but I might just manage to survive. Now if you'd
like to go and change after finishing that glass of wine,
I'll have another ready when you come down and we
can have an hour ignoring each other before lunch.
OK?'

'You really are the most manipulating, conniving,
scheming——'

'True, true.' He waved a languid hand in her direction. 'But don't waste all that precious energy that
you seem in such short supply of by taxing your brain
unnecessarily, my little firecracker.'

He didn't open his eyes when she returned to the
garden, this time clad in a one-piece swimming
costume that seemed a little more circumspect than
the very brief bikini she had bought in the Caribbean

on her honeymoon and which Blade loved. She
lowered herself gingerly on to the sun-lounger,
reaching out for the glass of wine and drinking half
of it before she realised what she had done. Nearly
two glasses on an empty stomach and it was potent
stuff. She felt the effects making her head swim a little.
Blade only bought the best, and this particular wine
was nectar. Another little ploy? she thought balefully
as she glanced across at the big male body at her side.
Probably. This wasn't Blade Forbes, devoted husband
any longer, this was Blade Forbes, adversary, and she
had better remember it.

But he did look good. She found she couldn't tear
her eyes away from the broad muscled shoulders and
powerful chest, the dark, curling body hair causing
her lower stomach to tighten in response as her eyes
followed its progress down into the hidden contours
of his groin. He really was film star material.

The thought sparked memory of a little forgotten
incident on their honeymoon when she had heard a
young teenager gabbling excitedly to her friend as
Blade and herself had walked down the gangplank of
Blade's friends' fabulous yacht in the South of France.

'That couple there, look.' The stage whisper had
easily carried to Amy's sharp ears, although Blade
was exchanging careless banter over his shoulder with
his friend at the time and had been oblivious of the
little scene. 'I'm sure they must be famous, film stars
or something. He's such a hunk and she's lovely, look
at that skin and hair.' Amy had almost turned to see
who they were talking about before she caught herself
in time, her cheeks flushing pink. 'And that boat...'
The girl's voice had been green with envy. 'Shall we

ask for their autographs? This package tour has cost us enough, we might as well make the most of it.'

'Don't be daft.' The girl's less effusive friend had hung back in alarm. 'You don't do that here, our Tracy. Anyway, you're not sure who they are, they might just be ordinary people like us.'

'Like us?' Tracy's voice had dripped contempt. 'Oh, come on, Shirl, there's nothing ordinary about people like that.'

Later, in the privacy of their cabin after a long languid night of making love, she had told Blade about the conversation, expecting him to laugh, but he had raised her chin gently to take her lips in a long, lingering kiss as dawn broke through the cabin window. 'They're dead right,' he said softly as his eyes had caressed her naked body sensually, 'there is nothing ordinary about you, my love. Me?' He had shrugged big shoulders dismissively. 'Ten a penny in this place but I haven't seen another woman who can even begin to compete with you. And the crazy thing is you don't rate your beauty at all, do you? Why, angel-face?'

And that had been the point when she had first brought herself to lay open the wound that had seared so deep to another human being's gaze. She had poured out the misery of her childhood, Sandra's rejection, the constant feeling that she had to apologise every minute for how she looked. And Blade had listened. And then he had made love to her, slowly, completely, in a way he never had before, that had taken them both to heaven and back. And afterwards he had talked to her for hours until the sun was a bright white ball in the transparent blue sky outside, and she had felt the burden leave her shoulders as she had laid it on his.

'A dime for them?' She hadn't been aware that he was watching her but now, as the deep blue of her eyes focused on the dark glittering black of his she realised that her face had been open for him to read.

'Not worth it,' she answered quietly as she forced the past back into the past, letting her hair hide her face quickly, far more shaken by the starkly beautiful memories than she would have liked. They had been so happy, so wildly, dangerously happy, she should have known it was too good to last.

'Liar.' He grimaced cynically. 'But I promised you an hour's peace, so stretch out there in comfort and take in some rays. And I don't want to hear mention of a certain man's name; it's just you and me, Amy. Got it?' The thread of steel underlying the mocking tone told her he meant every word literally. 'I'll wake you at lunchtime.'

'I didn't know you could cook?' she asked as she did as he'd bid, feeling her head reel a little as she lay back on the warm cushioned bed.

'There are a lot of things you don't know about me, sweetheart,' he said smoothly, 'but we won't go into that now.'

'Why?' She shut her eyes against the harsh glare of the sun, feeling its warmth caress her body and ease the tenseness out of her muscles. Blade was right, this did feel good.

'Because you wouldn't like it,' he said harshly. 'I don't know what sort of guy you thought I was, Amy, but I sure as hell don't let go of what is mine so easy

as you'd hoped. I want——' He stopped abruptly.
'Well, let's forget that now. As I said, relax, enjoy...'

Enjoy? Her nerves were as tight as a coiled spring
again as she forced herself to lie absolutely still, her
eyes closed. There had been such naked fury in his
voice those last few moments, such explosive rage.
He hadn't given up. She had been crazy to think he
had. He wouldn't rest until she was crushed and
broken at his feet with her soul laid bare. That was
what he wanted, she thought painfully as the wine
heightened her emotions. Revenge for her supposed
betrayal of their marriage, retribution for all the
misery she had caused...

She must have slept, because as she became aware
of sensual lips on hers the sensation had a dream-like
quality to it, a satisfyingly safe fantasy where all her
deepest needs and desires could be given free rein.
She opened her mouth hungrily, seeking more from
the deliciously warm illusion that was appeasing the
fierce longing that was with her every waking moment,
her lips murmuring the name that haunted even her
dreams. 'Blade...' The smell, the feel of him, it was
all there. She ran her fingers lightly down the hard
male body poised over hers before opening her eyes
drowsily as the drugged inertia began to recede.

'Blade!' This time his name sprang from her lips
in shock as her heavy eyelids were forced wide open,
and she confronted his face an inch from hers, a look
of immense satisfaction lighting the chiselled features. 'What are you doing!'

'I would have thought that was pretty obvious,' he
drawled lazily as his hands continued their dizzying

wander over her body. 'I'm calling you to lunch, of course.'

'Lunch?' She shuddered deeply as his hands drifted slowly over her flat stomach, smothering the sound of pleasure that rose into her throat. 'I don't understand...' For a moment she couldn't remember where she was and then, as her senses returned and she took in the sights and smells of the garden, she sat up jerkily, almost knocking Blade off the lounger as he crouched over her on his knees. 'Will you stop that!' She knocked his hands away from her in a desperate gesture of repudiation.

'Sure.' He had frozen at the none-too-subtle rejection, his eyes icing over and his body tensing, and as he stood upright she saw his face had hardened, a derisively cruel gleam darkening the beautiful eyes. 'I only intended a waking kiss after all, sweetheart; it was your reaction that set the ball rolling.'

'I don't know what you mean.' She stared at him, mortified, as he laughed softly, the sound chilling.

'No?' He glanced at her body which mirrored her mind's betrayal, her breasts hard and pointed and straining against the thin cloth, her skin flushed and warm and aroused. 'Who's kidding who, Amy?'

'I was asleep.' She felt her lips tremble at his contempt and tried desperately not to let it show. 'I was dreaming.'

'Amy.' His quick eyes had caught her distress and now all mockery was gone as he knelt at her side, his gaze searching her face with an intensity that was unnerving. 'It's not wrong to respond to your husband, is it? Even before we were married I wouldn't have called you frigid or inhibited—what the hell has happened to you, woman? It's as though——' He stopped abruptly and shook his head as he stood up again slowly, his face dark and grim. 'It's as though you're forcing yourself to hate me. Why?' he asked harshly.

'It's not like that.' She swung her legs over the side of the lounger, letting her hair shimmer into a golden curtain between them. 'You don't understand.'

'I sure as hell don't,' he agreed on a small snarl that sent a shiver down her spine. She knew that if she looked up his face would be bitter and cold, and who could blame him? she asked herself painfully. Did he love her any more? A tight band constricted her chest, stopping her breath. Probably not, she acknowledged with agonising honesty. How could he after all that had happened? But he still desired her physically and that was almost as dangerous.

'You said something about lunch?' She couldn't bear to raise her head and see his face as she spoke the trite words. 'I'm starving.'

There was a long minute of silence and then his voice came from above her head, cold and controlled. 'So am I,' he said expressionlessly, and as she followed him into the cottage it came to her, on a little stab of fear, that he hadn't been talking about the roast beef dinner laid out on the small kitchen table.

CHAPTER EIGHT

'WOTCHER, darlin'' Amy turned quickly to confront the bunch of leather-clad youths who had just driven open the door of the restaurant with unnecessary force. 'Got any leftovers, then?'

'We're just closing.' She stitched a polite smile on her face with some effort as she pointed to the small sign at the side of the front window. 'We don't take orders after ten.'

'Well, that's a shame, ain't it, Mick?'

Mick gave a vacant leering smile as he nodded agreement without taking his eyes off Amy, his ginger hair thick with grease.

'Cause we're a bit thirsty, see? The lads fancied a cup of coffee and a doughnut or somethin'. Didn't you, lads?' The speaker was a massive burly man of about twenty who looked as though most of his brains resided in the part of his anatomy that rested on the seat of the monstrous motorbike he had parked outside. 'An' they can get a bit naughty, like, if they don't get what they want.'

'Amy?' Arthur had obviously caught the tail-end of the conversation as he stepped through from the kitchen, and his voice was placatory as he nodded at the group who had seated themselves sprawlingly at the table by the window. 'I think we've got some doughnuts in the back and the coffee pot is still on.'

He motioned for her to take his place in the kitchen.
'All right lads?'

'Yeah, jump to it, girl.'

He obviously fancied himself as something of a wit,
Amy thought tightly as she flashed one scathing glance
at the boy who had been doing all the talking before
walking thankfully through into the kitchen to the
sound of the group's bawdy mocking laughter. This
was all she needed! She closed her eyes tightly in
protest for one second before putting a batch of
doughnuts hastily into the microwave as she switched
on the coffee again.

'Sorry about that, lass, but I thought it better to
humour them.' Arthur had followed on her heels, his
face worried. 'Is John picking you up tonight?'

'No.' She glanced at the restaurant door nervously.
'I told him not to.' She'd thought that wise in case
Blade was around but now...

'A pity.' Arthur peered anxiously out of the glass
panel of the kitchen door before taking the doughnuts
out of the microwave and covering them liberally in
sugar. 'I've an idea they are the bunch who were down
this way last summer and caused all the trouble. Hung
about for a few days bothering all the lasses and being
generally obnoxious, and then old Charlie got
involved.'

'Charlie?' Amy stared at him. 'I don't know a
Charlie?'

'You wouldn't now.' Arthur's face was grim. 'He
was the village copper, great bloke, one of a kind. He
made them move on one night, and the next he was
attacked by persons unknown. Beat him uncon-
scious, they did, and left him in a pool of blood

outside the Flying Duck. He's been in hospital ever since, can't walk or talk.'

'Oh, Arthur.' Amy's face turned white. 'What are we going to do?'

'Now I didn't say it was them as did it, lass,' Arthur said quickly as he took in her blanched face. 'Charlie's never been able to say who and that lot had disappeared by then. There were a group of travellers passing through and they were questioned for days, but in the end they had to let 'em go, no evidence. But all the folks round here come to their own conclusion, so they did.' He nodded slowly. 'So you just stay in here, lass, and I'll see to 'em.'

'All right, Arthur.' Amy quickly placed five cups of coffee and the doughnuts on a tray and handed it to him with shaking hands. 'Be careful.'

As Arthur disappeared into the adjoining room she heard the ribald comments get positively obscene, and tensed in fright as she heard her name. 'Where's the lovely Amy, then?' a slurred voice shouted suggestively. 'Looks like she might do a turn, that one?'

'That's enough of that.' Arthur re-appeared through the door as he spoke. 'Just calm down, lads, we don't want no trouble, do we?' He gestured to the phone on the kitchen wall with his eyes. 'Dial 999, Amy, lass,' he whispered softly. 'I think we're going to have some bother.'

She had just finished making the call when the kitchen door swung open and two of the youths entered slowly, their mean little eyes bright and hot as they glanced from her frightened face to Arthur's grim one. 'More coffee, Grandpop.' They indicated the pot of coffee on the table. 'And this time *she* can bring it out.'

'Amy's working in here.' Arthur's face was set and cold, all trace of appeasement gone. 'I'll see to you.'

'Are you deaf as well as stupid, old man?' Before Amy had time to react, the other three youths had followed their comrades in, two of them hoisting Arthur bodily out of the door and seating him in a chair as one of the others forced Amy into the restaurant. 'We'll let you watch, Grandpop.' As the blinds went down over the windows Amy knew such fear that her heart stopped beating and then she screamed, desperately, before a large dirty hand was clamped like iron over her mouth.

'Shut her up.' The spokesman's face was vicious. 'Gag her or something. She might make a lot more noise before we've finished.' He dropped the latch on the door as he spoke and then turned, gesturing at the two holding Arthur down in the seat. 'Keep hold of him. Any trouble, hit him hard. An' you, mister.' He pushed his sweaty face close to Arthur's. 'Just remember that when we do a job we make sure it's a good one. Like last summer. Know what I mean?'

'Shut up, Beef.' One of the youths, a little younger and cleaner than the rest, glanced nervously at his leader. 'We got away with that, don't——'

The rest of his warning was lost as the locked door of the restaurant flew open with such an almighty bang that for a second Amy thought one of the boys had fired a gun. And then she saw Blade standing in the doorway, his glittering eyes taking in the scene in front of him with one piercing glance, the look on his face chilling.

'Let go of her.' His voice was like the snarl of a
wild beast, and for a moment the filthy hands gripping
her so hard slackened before tightening even harder.

'Oh, yeah, says who?' The one they'd called Beef
spoke to the youth directly behind him without taking
his eyes off Blade. 'Hold on to the old man and don't
stand no aggro. Me an' Flick'll deal with this Yankee.'

As she saw one of the teenagers tighten his grip into
a stranglehold round Arthur's neck, she was also
aware of Blade striking with sudden deadly force at
the youth nearest to him who went down like a stone,
but events were happening so fast it was a kaleido-
scope of sound and colour.

Part of her couldn't believe it *was* happening. It
was the sort of incident one read about in the papers,
maybe describing a relatively normal occurrence in
the inner cities or the depths of the Glasgow slums
where drug-pushers and mindless bored hooligans
were all too common, but here? In this sleepy
Yorkshire village?

And then Arthur slumped forward in his seat,
whether from the pressure on his windpipe or his heart
she didn't know, and as the youth who had been
holding him leapt into the fray Amy realised Blade
didn't stand a chance. He was going to be badly hurt,
like Charlie, and there was nothing she could do about
it.

It could only have been another minute before the
harsh sound of a police siren registered on her frantic
senses, but in that time she had realised that Blade
hadn't learnt his fighting techniques solely in the
boardroom. Marquis of Queensberry didn't come into
it. For every dirty trick the group of youths pulled he

had one to match it, and as the three who were still on their feet tried to make their escape as two police cars screeched to a halt outside, the one who had been holding her giving her a vicious push against the wall as he did so, Blade moved into the doorway his eyes murderous.

'Try it, just try it.' He had fixed his deadly gaze on Beef's mean little eyes and now beckoned to the huge youth, giving a snarl of a smile as he did so. 'Come on, I'd like you to. There must be a lot of people out there who owe you one.'

'Flick?' As Beef reached behind him with his hand outstretched Amy realised the portent of the other lad's nickname, as a vicious-looking flick knife appeared as though by magic in Beef's great paw.

'Blade!' As she screamed his name it took his attention just long enough for Beef to seize the advantage, leaping forward and slicing through the air with the wickedly sharp knife as he did so. Blade's reflexes were as finely honed as a big cat's and almost certainly saved his life, and as he kicked the knife out of harm's way she saw Beef's eyes open very wide in desperate panic. And then Blade hit him, very hard, and he was out for the count, sprawling to the floor as the police surged through the door. It was over.

'Amy? Sit down. Put your head between your knees.' She had stood up to go to Blade's side, but as the room had begun to swim and turn he was there in front of her, forcing her down in a chair as he gestured to Arthur, who seemed to have recovered, to hold on to her. 'I'll get some brandy.' He was back in an instant, forcing the liquid down her throat as he held the glass to her lips, and not moving away until she had taken several helpless gulps.

'Blade... If you hadn't come in...'

'But I did, didn't I?' he said gently, as he searched the white face and dilated eyes. 'I'll always be there when you need me, Amy, don't you know that by now? I love you, I'll always love you, nothing you can do or say will make any difference to that.'

She stared up at him, her face stricken. 'Blade——'

'I'm sorry, sir, but we are going to have to ask you a few questions if the lady is up to it?' A young policeman, who couldn't have been more than twenty-one, stood apologetically at their side, and as Blade turned irritably to face him Amy put her hand on his sleeve, noticing as she did so that it was stained with blood. His or theirs? she thought, as her stomach lurched sickeningly.

'Yes, of course,' she said quickly. 'I'd rather get it over and done with now.'

It was another half hour before the police were satisfied, and by then Amy could see that Blade was in some considerable pain. 'It's all right.' He had caught her gaze on him as he winced on standing up, his face immediately straightening. 'Just a few cuts and bruises, but I think a couple of the other guys came off worse.' She couldn't respond to the lightness, her face whitening still more as she noticed one bronzed cheekbone was already turning blue.

'I'd take her home, lad.' Arthur was his normal stolid self although his voice was still croaky. No one had mentioned his passing out; Amy had an idea the blunt old Yorkshireman would rather die than ac-

knowledge it. 'Good night's sleep and the world will
be a different place.'

A different place? Amy had the insane feeling that
she was going to shout and scream and throw herself
on the floor, as a combination of shock and bitter
pain swept over her in a black flood. If only Arthur
knew. He thought this was the worst thing that had
happened to her? She closed her eyes against the
thought. How she wished it were. If she could leave
this place with Blade as his wife and go back to their
own home with nothing more serious than Beef's disgusting image in her mind, how grateful she would
be. A desolation too great for words filled her soul,
and then she reached out beyond herself for strength
and composure to get through the next few minutes.

'That's not necessary.' She tried to smile, but found
it was beyond her. 'One of the policemen said he
would take me home.'

'I'm taking you home,' Blade said tonelessly, his
eyes veiled as she glanced his way. 'And don't argue,
Amy, not tonight, not now.' There was something in
the complete lack of expression in both face and voice
that stopped the protest she had been about to make
more effectively than anything else could have done.

'All right.' Her voice was small. 'I'll get my jacket.'
One thing was blazing in her mind above anything
else as they walked out to the car. He could have been
killed tonight and it would have been through pro-
tecting her. It would have been *her* fault. Somehow
she shouldn't have put herself in that position, she
should have known better. Perhaps something she had
said or done had made the gang act as they did? She
just didn't know any more. Perhaps her aunt and uncle

had been right after all, that she was bad, vile, a snare
to trip men up and bring out the beast in them?

She brushed her hair back from her face with a
weary hopeless gesture as she slipped into the car. She
was so tired, so deathly tired and everything had gone
so horribly wrong...

'Don't start thinking any of that was your fault.'
He had read her mind, but she should have expected
it, she thought miserably. His discernment was terrifying. 'Those animals are not fit to draw breath. In
every generation a few foul specimens like that rear
their heads, but thankfully they are few and far between. They see something beautiful and they want
to possess and destroy. They'll never be any good for
anything.'

His voice was icy cold with contempt, and she remembered with a little shiver how he had moved very
close to Beef as two policemen had frogmarched the
sullen youth out of the door. 'Just a minute.' His face
had been on a level with the scowling countenance in
front of him and his voice had been low and rapier-
sharp. 'If you ever, *ever*, come near me or mine again,
I shall make you wish you'd never been born. Got
it?' He moved a shade nearer, his eyes blazing. 'But
I shall do it my way, understand? And my fingers
reach a very long way indeed, sonny. The world
wouldn't be big enough for you to hide. And you'd
want to hide.' The twist to his lips couldn't have been
described as a smile. 'You'd pray that you could hide.
To be locked away somewhere safe would seem sweet.'

The police had looked less than thrilled at the
blatant threat, and Beef and his cronies hadn't looked

too pleased either as they had left, almost dragging the policemen with them.

'Would you really hurt them, Blade? If they came back?' She looked at him quietly.

'Yes.' He spared her a fleeting glance as he started the powerful engine. 'I didn't grow up in an American mining town without learning a few nasty tricks, Amy, and also making the odd dubious contact. Now I'm not particularly proud of that part of my life, but if I have to use it to protect what's mine I'll do so.' He smiled grimly. 'But they won't be back. Beef is just crazy enough to recognise someone more crazy than himself. And I was crazy tonight. When I saw that slug holding you——' He stopped abruptly. 'Let's say I'd have done whatever was necessary, and leave it at that.'

'I'm sorry, Blade.' Her voice was a small painful whisper, and he shook his head irritably as he negotiated a difficult bend.

'There's no need, get that into your head. You didn't do anything wrong. Forget all the rubbish you were fed before you met me, and trust me. I don't know what's going on in that head of yours some of the time, but one thing I do know. None of this was your fault. What you're feeling now, thousands of other victims of mindless violence have felt. That they somehow contributed to the circumstances. That they should have been somewhere else, acted differently, dressed differently, whatever. It's rubbish. You were innocent, totally innocent, and they acted out of their own greed and darkness. You understand me? *Do you understand me, Amy*?' The last words demanded a reply, and she nodded weakly.

'If you say so.'

'Good girl.' His eyes flashed over her white face before returning to the dark road. 'I'm taking you back to my place for the night, OK? I'll sleep on the couch if that makes you feel better.' It didn't, but she dared not say so. 'Do you want to talk this thing through?'

She had the feeling that he was talking of more than just the night's happenings and shook her head shakily. 'No. I want to forget it.'

He said no more, concentrating on the short ride home through the sleeping countryside that was still and dark. Was it only yesterday that he had cooked her Sunday lunch? she asked herself incredulously as they turned off the main lane into the little sandy track that led to Blade's cottage. A lunch that had ended so disastrously, with Blade leaving in icy silence as soon as they had eaten and her sitting in numb frozen stillness all the long hot afternoon? How long could they carry on like this, on this emotional see-saw that continued to empty and fill her until she thought she would explode with the intensity of her heartache? And there was no escape. Not now. Not ever. The best, and worst, that she could hope for was that he would leave her alone.

'Out you get.' She could tell from his voice that he was trying to be cool and brisk, to give an air of normality to an evening that had anything but. 'I think a cup of coffee liberally laced with brandy is in order, don't you? Perhaps you'd see to it while I change my shirt.' She looked at the one he was wearing, torn and stained with blood, and felt sick again as he opened the door to the cottage and waved her in.

'Blade——' She stopped abruptly as he swung round, his eyes enquiring. He was so handsome, so strong in mind and body, she loved him so much . . . 'I think you should bathe that bruise on your face. Your eye is almost closed.'

'No problem.' He dismissed the battered state of his face with careless disregard.

'No, please.' She caught hold of his arm. 'You sit down and I'll get some water and a towel. You'll have to have a bath and soak all the rest of your injuries later; you're going to be black and blue.'

'I'm not going to argue if you want to fuss a bit over me,' he said with the quirky smile she loved so much. 'I've missed it.'

She turned away quickly, the lump in her throat threatening to choke her, finding once she was in the kitchen that she had to unclench her hands from the tight fists they had knotted into before she could collect what she needed.

As she went back into the room the very air was vibrating, the silence loud and deafening, and as she knelt in front of him and gently touched the cold flannel to his swollen face she found she was praying desperately, a soundless blind prayer that she wouldn't betray herself, that she would be strong, that——

'Kiss me.'

'What?' His eyes had been closed, but now they were open and staring straight into hers, dark and glittering.

'I said kiss me.' As she remained frozen in front of him, his eyes softened and turned warm and meltingly gentle. 'Please.'

And so she did what she knew she mustn't do, what
she wanted to do, what she ached and longed to do,
touching her lips to the swollen taut skin under his
eye and tracing a path across the hard tanned face to
his waiting mouth. And he kissed her back, wildly,
frantically, like a man dying of thirst at the fountain
of life. And after that there was no going back.

At first his hunger made him almost savage as his
mouth devoured hers, bruising and crushing her lips
until she thought she would cry out, and then the
control he had always drawn on re-emerged, and his
mouth became warm and sensuously erotic, helping
his hands bring her body to glorious life as he gently
stripped the clothes from her body and then his own.

She froze, just for a second, as she saw the marks
on his body that the gang's fists and boots had inflicted, and then he smothered her pale limbs with his
own, soothing her, touching her, until nothing else
mattered in the world but the two of them and the
sensations he was bringing forth out of her aching
form. The riptide of pleasure was impossible to fight,
her pale, almost translucent, skin a stark contrast to
the tanned hardness of his, her full breasts, heavy with
passion, wonderfully aroused against the coarse tight
body hair that covered his powerful chest.

How had she managed so long without him? As
his mouth and tongue made searingly sensual assaults
on every part of her body, she ran her fingers over
the warm male flesh that was so completely hers. He
was hers. The knowledge was traitorously exhilar-
ating. From the first moment they had met he had
been hers. As she had been his. He meant more than
life itself.

At the moment of possession she was pierced through, for one brief second, with an emotion of such feverish joy and sadness that she cried his name out loud, and then they continued into the heights together as he murmured her name over and over again in an agony of love.

And then, when it was over, he cradled her close against the comforting bulk of his body, wrapping his arms and legs round her as though to protect her from all the world could inflict, never knowing that what attacked her was from within. She found she couldn't talk or think, sinking into the deep blanket of sleep as she lay enfolded in his arms, her mind dulled and still, and just content to be held next to the man she loved so much.

She wasn't sure what woke her from the thick dreamless lethargy, but she found her eyes were heavy and tired as though she had been drugged. Blade was still asleep, his body curved around her and his limbs acting both as a shield and a cover.

For a moment the languor was too deep, too somnolent for her to raise herself, and then a burning stream of hot self-loathing flooded her limbs with pure adrenalin. How could she have been so weak, so criminally, stupidly weak? All the weeks of heartache, all the bitter confrontations and painful rows—and for what? She was back where she had been three months ago, about to break his heart for a second time, but this time things would be so much worse. She had run away, and that hadn't worked. She had tried rejecting him, and look where that had got her. What could she do? *What could she do?*

'Amy, darling…' As Blade stirred and then opened his eyes, she saw his face was open and unguarded, his eyes hungry for her. 'Everything will be all right, sweetheart.'

She stiffened, her whole body tensing at what she must do. But could she do it? Could she convince him after what they had just shared that it was all a mistake? A physical weakness momentarily appeased. Could she?

CHAPTER NINE

'BLADE, I have to go.' She jerked out of his arms with such force that she heard his elbow crack against the floor through the thick sheepskin rug on which they had lain. 'I must get back.'

'There's no rush.' His voice was lazy, warm. 'We've the whole night——'

'No!' She was already pulling on her clothes with feverish haste, and this time the tone of her voice got through to him as he raised himself slowly on one elbow, his face hardening.

'Not again. For crying out loud, not again.'

'You don't understand.' She heard him move, a rustle of clothes, a zip fastening into place, and then he was in front of her clad only in his jeans, his face more angry than she had ever seen it, his black eyes blazing like an inferno.

'I'm going to.' His voice was low and tight, the same voice he had used to Beef in the restaurant. 'Believe me, Amy, I'm going to. No more evasions, no more double talk. You are going to talk to me tonight, really talk——'

'You can't make me!' She could hear the hysteria in her voice herself, and winced at the shrillness even as she recognised that she was frightened. Badly frightened. The coldly dangerous man standing in front of her was at the end of his tether; even if she hadn't loved him so much she would have known that.

'I can make you, and you know it.' In contrast to
her voice, his had got lower, the deepness chilling her
bones. 'Why did you leave, Amy? And don't give me
that garbage about it not working. That wasn't the
reason was it? *Was it*?' The last two words had been
like pistol shots in her ears and she jumped visibly,
taking a step backwards as she gazed up at him with
huge drowning eyes. 'I'm prepared to stay here for
days, weeks, months, until I get an answer. And this
John!' He dismissed poor John with an angry jab of
his hand. 'You don't care for him. You couldn't make
love with me the way we've just done if you did. I
know you, Amy. *I know you*. Try and tell me you
don't love me! Tell me you want me out of your life
for good.'

She put her hand to her mouth as he moved a step
towards her, for all the world like a huge dark avenging
angel that was going to tear her heart out by its roots.
And then it was all too much. Before he could stop
her she had fled towards the door, pulling it open and
rushing out into the dark night as though she had
wings on her feet. She had to get away. Had to
escape . . .

He caught her before she had even left the per-
imeter of the house, pulling her round with such force
that she felt her head spin as he shook her hard. 'You
will tell me! Now! I love you, I have the right to know!
You're my *wife*, damn it. What about all the plans
we made? Children. A house in the country. Growing
old together——'

'I'll never grow old!' She was screaming, over and
over again, all the pent-up emotion of months
breaking forth as she gave up the fight to be brave,

to be strong. 'I won't, do you hear! At the most I've got just a few years before this body begins to break down, to decay, to give up! And then I'll be on crutches, and then a wheelchair——'

'Amy!'

'No, you listen to me! This is what you wanted, isn't it, to hear it all? Well, you've got what you wanted! I'm telling you now——'

The slap across her face was just hard enough to break the frenzied hysteria that had brought a red mist before her eyes, and as his dark face swam into focus she was suddenly enfolded in his arms as he lifted her bodily and strode back into the house. She didn't try to struggle against his superior strength, there was no point, and besides she felt numb and lifeless as the enormity of what she had done washed over her. A living hell. She had condemned him to a living hell. If the knowledge of what was going to happen was too hard for him to bear and he left her, he would carry the guilt with him for the rest of his life. If he stayed—her mind slammed to a halt. What had she done? How could she have told him if she really loved him? And she did, so much.

'Relax, baby, relax . . .' He was holding her in the chair now, crooning softly as he smothered her face in tiny comforting kisses that held none of the previous passion in their depths. 'It'll be all right, I promise you——'

'It won't, Blade.' The strength to speak came from somewhere and she swallowed deeply as she raised herself just enough to look into his face, seeing the hard features and dark eyes that were soft and des-

perate with love with a mad pounding of her heart.
'It can't be.'

Now she did struggle to get down, but he drew her
tightly against him, so close she could hear the crazy
throbbing of his heart that belied the outward composure. 'Whatever this is we'll face it together, my
love, now——'

'Blade, I've got a disease that is going to kill me
slowly over a period of years,' she said with icy
numbness, her body as stiff as a board. This time he
allowed her to draw away just a little so she could
look right into his face, and what she saw shattered
the numbness into a million tiny pieces. His face was
as white as a sheet, his eyes stricken. 'I won't be
beautiful any more, I won't be anything. I won't be
able to walk at first, then other muscles will begin to
be affected and eventually——' She stopped abruptly
and then forced herself to go on. 'Eventually I'll be
bedridden on a machine and then I'll die.'

'Stop it.' He shook her gently, his hands warm on
her cold flesh. 'Don't talk like this.'

'But it's the truth, Blade. You wanted the truth and
now you've got it.' She should never have told him.
Her mind was screaming denunciation at her. He
wouldn't be able to cope with this thing, why should
he? It wasn't his problem; in all he had only known
her for just twelve months. It wasn't fair to expect
him to give up years of his life too when he could be
free and happy and——

'Why didn't you tell me?' he asked quietly. 'What
have I ever done to you, Amy, that you couldn't tell
me?' The words seemed torn out of his very soul.
'Didn't you trust me at all?'

'I love you, Blade,' she said dully.

'And that's an answer?' He was breathing hard, his voice husky. 'You love me and so you leave me? You take away the only thing that makes life worth living and you tell me that's love?'

'Blade——'

'No, you listen to me now.' He stood up with her in his arms, placing her feet on the ground as he took her forearms in his hands, and she could feel the shaking of his body even through her own trembling. 'When I came back and found that note I wanted to die.' His eyes held hers, piercingly dark, and the pain and hopelessness in their inky blackness chilled her bones. 'I didn't want to live, Amy. I would never have imagined a woman could do that to me before I met you, and when I did . . .' His voice trailed away for a moment, and then he continued slowly, 'When I did meet you I knew I could trust you completely, I *knew* it.'

She stared up at him, incapable of speech.

'But you couldn't trust *me*.' He took a long deep breath. 'Why?'

'It wasn't that——'

'The hell it wasn't.' He wasn't shouting, but the pain in his voice was more agonising than any rage. 'You ran away, you didn't give me a chance, and you faced this thing all on your own. You shut me out, Amy . . .'

'But the flowers,' she whispered slowly. 'It wasn't fair to ask you to accept this when you felt that way. I didn't want you to pity me, I didn't want to disgust you——'

'What other world have you been in?' he asked
tautly. 'How can you even think for one minute...'
He pulled her to him with such violent suddenness
that her hair flew out behind her in a golden arc, and
then his mouth descended on hers for one blindingly
sweet moment before he put her away from him again.
'We have to talk.' He eyed her tensely. 'And this time
I want everything. But first——' he sat her down in
a chair and moved to kneel in front of her, his eyes
holding hers with such gentleness that she began to
cry without even knowing it '—first I must tell you
how it is, my darling. I love you. I love you more than
anything or anyone and I always will. If this disease
takes you, if we can't find a cure——' she moved to
speak but he put his hand to her mouth '—then I'll
die too. Oh, I might go on living for another ten,
twenty, thirty years but I'll be dead. And if you left
me *now* that's how it would be.'

'You'd get over me——'

'As you would me?' That thought had never occurred to her and she stared at him horror-stricken.
'Well, would you, *could* you?'

'No,' she whispered faintly.

'But I am supposed to recover?' There was a faint
touch of anger in his voice that he was trying to
control. 'Why? Because I'm a man? Or because you
don't think I really love you?'

'I know you love me,' she said weakly, her chest
aching as though she had been punched hard time
and time again. 'But to ask you to face this when you
don't have to——'

'The hell I don't.' He stared at her as though she
were mad. 'Where are you coming from, sweetheart?

From the first day I met you you became my life. You are *me*, Amy, don't you see? A part of me. We aren't two people any more. I can't separate myself from the tiniest thing that concerns you. I breathe you, sleep you...' His voice was a groan now, and she felt the blood racing through her veins as the tears ran unheeded down her face. 'You're my other half, the female part of me. You know how I think, what I feel——' He stopped abruptly. 'Or I thought you did. Maybe I went too fast too soon. I hadn't allowed for just how deep all the old insecurities had bitten. And what the hell have flowers to do with any of this?' he asked suddenly.

'At home,' she whispered, her lip trembling helplessly. 'You had to have them perfect, without blemish. You didn't like decay, you *told* me so,' she finished desperately as all the old dread reared its head again. 'New ones all the time——'

'Amy, those are *flowers*.' He shook his head slowly. 'What on earth had my idiosyncrasy about the damn flowers got to do with anything?'

'But I thought——' she couldn't bear to look at him and shut her eyes tightly '—I thought you would find it too hard to cope with seeing me slowly get ill. Sandra said——'

'Sandra?' He eyed her darkly as he forced her chin up, her eyes opening to meet his. 'I might have known. What has your damn sister got to do with this?'

'She's...' She took a deep breath and started again. 'You don't understand, Blade. She's ill. Terribly ill. As I'll be in a few years' time when I reach her age. She said I'll be a millstone round your neck and she's right. You have your own life to live——'

'I've never heard such callous rubbish in my life,'
he said furiously, his voice low and tight. 'I can't believe you really accepted that line of reasoning. What
the hell happened to our relationship, the trust, the
promise to love in sickness and in health? You think
I value you like the damn flowers? Is that it? That
I'd simply replace you with a fresh substitute and carry
on as normal? Is that really all you think of me?'

She stared at him blindly. Had she thought that?
No, not really, not at the very bottom of her, she
realised now.

'I love you, Amy.' He took her in his arms again
and stood silently as they swayed slowly back and
forth in an agony of grief. 'I'll always love you
whether we're together or apart. When you're not with
me the world is grey, empty. Damn it!' His arms closed
tighter until she could hardly breathe. 'Of course I
think you're beautiful because you are, but that's only
a tiny part of it. I love *you*, the person under the skin
and hair and bones. I love your strength of mind,
your honesty, your sense of humour, all the things
that make you you. If you had an accident tomorrow
and were horribly disfigured or hurt, of course I'd
care, I'd care like hell, but not in the way you seem
to think. It would hurt me because it hurt you, but
we'd face it together. Now you are going to sit down
and tell me it all, from the beginning, starting with
the day I left on that France trip.'

'Are you sure you really want to know?' she asked
tremulously as he pulled her down on to his lap as he
sat in the chair. 'Everything is cut and dried; there's
no chance of a reprieve or that it's curable. I wouldn't
blame you if you wanted to leave——'

'Well, I'd sure blame you,' he said grimly. 'You're mine, Amy, and I'm yours. I have the right to expect everything from you that I wouldn't even want from anyone else, love, fidelity, the whole caboodle——'

'And there'll be no family, no children,' she said quietly, as she felt something begin to rise in her, a flood of pain and joy and anguish that constricted her chest in a tight band. 'It's hereditary, you see, in baby girls. I couldn't risk——'

'You're my family,' he said softly, his eyes gentle. 'I told you that when we were first married when I explained about Mom and my father and Todd. If it's just you, and no kids, then I'll take that and be damn grateful——'

As the flood finally tore out of her she shook them both with her sobs, the months of heartache and loneliness and black terror escaping from her eyes and nose and mouth in a torrent of weeping that filled the small room with its agony, and he was wise enough to let her cry for long, long minutes as he held her close to his heart.

And later, as they talked, he still held her close as though he would never be able to make up for all those lost days and nights when they could have been together. She told him it all and the sun was finally rising in the small copse behind the house before she had finished.

And then they went to bed, to love and touch and feel until that same sun was a high golden ball in the flawless blue of the sky and the sunlight flooded rich and bright into the tiny bedroom where she lay wrapped in his arms as they both slept.

And much later, as evening shadows coloured the room a soft grey, he explained about the flowers, his voice painful and taut. 'My father never brought flowers or any little gift to Mom while he was alive. Todd and I used to pick bunches of wild lilies and buttercups on our way home from school sometimes, and her face used to light up. She'd keep them until they were dead and faded before she could bear to throw them out. And later, when I had left home, I sent her a bouquet every week no matter where I was.' He stopped, his face constricting, and she hugged his bare chest tight as she gazed up into his face dark with memories.

'Don't go on, Blade, I don't care about the flowers——'

'No, I want to.' He glanced down at her lying by his side and smiled gently. 'I should have told you months ago but I still find it hard to talk about. I found her, you see. I'd called in on a flying visit for the weekend and she must have died the previous day, a heart attack, the post-mortem revealed. There were bouquets all around the room, old and dead and faded, with all the little cards in a pile. When I visited I never went in the bedroom and that's where she'd kept them, hordes of them.' He shook his head slowly. 'The sight of all those dead flowers with her lying there did something to me I'll never forget. And she looked so peaceful, even happy. The ultimate irony.'

'They must have given her a lot of joy,' Amy said softly as the picture he painted rent her heart.

'Yes, I suppose they did.' He wrinkled his brow as he moved restlessly. 'I never looked at it like that before. It just seemed so sad, such a waste of a life.'

'It just depends how you look at it,' she said quietly.

'So do lots of things.' He stroked the soft silk of her hair thoughtfully. 'Can we go home now? At last?'

'But Mrs Cox——'

'Has been in residence for the last twenty-four hours.' He looked down at her expressionlessly. 'That was what I had come to tell you last night. Arthur was going to ring her after we'd left and explain you were with me.'

'You never said.' She wriggled slightly in his arms. 'I could have gone back there last night.'

'Over my dead body,' he said grimly. 'I had the sense to realise I wouldn't get another chance like that one to get to the bottom of things.'

'You took advantage of a situation like that?' she began indignantly, even as a small smile touched her mouth.

'Too true.' The dark deep voice held no remorse whatsoever. 'I was getting desperate. And now you're coming home, Mrs Forbes, where you belong. But first . . .'

This time he made love to her slowly, lingeringly, his eyes hot with passion and his big masculine body hard and commanding. She trembled at the feel of his skin next to hers, warm and pulsating, at the fierce need his mouth and hands were drawing from her quivering form. 'I could eat you alive . . .' His voice was a dark growl of passion. 'How could you have stopped me doing this for so long?' She tried to answer, to offer some solace, but in a few seconds no words were necessary as she melted into the exquisite fire that was consuming them both.

His mouth was flagrantly erotic, coaxing her on and on into new intimacies that she met eagerly, wantonly, her whole being concentrating wholly on the delicious sensations that had her trembling helplessly in his arms. The past, the future, counted as nothing. All that was real was Blade. Just Blade.

CHAPTER TEN

THEY had been home for three days when Blade had to leave on a trip he explained it was impossible to postpone. Their time together had been bittersweet, each moment intense and precious and threaded through with the knowledge that they had to compress a whole lifetime of loving into just a few short years.

Amy was sitting quietly in the garden in the evening shadows, the hub of London life barely reaching into the protected opulent grounds surrounding Blade's beautiful mansion except for the odd faint scream of a police siren now and again rising above the muted drone of the world outside. The thick warm air was heavy against her face and bare arms; it had been a baking hot day and the weather man had forecast more to follow.

She followed the progress of a busy little insect gathering pollen from a flowering bush nearby, its transparent wings a blur in the dusky air, with sleepy interest. It was strange, this feeling that seemed to have taken her over since she had lain the burden of her illness on Blade's shoulders. She wasn't exactly happy—the knowledge of what she had to face was still too new for that—but somehow a kind of acceptance had settled like a warm comforting blanket over the horror and pain, and with it the joy of living had been revived. She couldn't be sure of what the

future would hold, Blade had impressed that on her
time and time again, except that they would face it
together and for the moment that was enough.

She glanced at the delicate gold watch on her wrist
idly. Nine o'clock. Evening birdsong had started, the
pure loud notes of a missel-thrush competing with the
other resident birds that inhabited the vast grounds
of Blade's mansion. Blade would be home this time
tomorrow evening if all went well, but she was already
missing him desperately although he had only been
gone since six that morning. She shut her eyes as she
leant back in the huge cushioned cane chair, her
thoughts heavy and dreamy. He *loved* her. More than
she had ever imagined possible. There was no more
room for doubts or fears but she wished, oh, she
wished she wouldn't have to leave him alone so soon.
The next few years seemed a painfully short time. It
was the knowing that was so hard; if it had happened
suddenly, in an accident, then maybe...

'Hello, sleeping beauty.' The warm hard kiss
brought her instantly awake from the light doze she
had fallen into, and she opened dazed blue eyes to
stare straight into Blade's glittering gaze. 'Oh, Amy,
my love...' He had whisked her up from the chair,
and into his arms before she could speak, holding her
so tight as he whirled her round and round in a frenzy
of excitement that she felt she would faint if he didn't
stop.

'Blade, no more——' He cut short her protestation
with another kiss that was almost savage in its intensity before letting her slide on to her feet still in
his arms. 'You aren't supposed to be home till tomorrow.' She stared at him anxiously. He looked

strange, wild, as though something was burning inside that was going to explode.

'I've got something to tell you.' His voice was shaking but the look on his face reassured the sudden panic that gripped her throat for a second. It couldn't be bad news, not with him looking like that. 'Sit down, you'll have to be sitting down, and let me finish before you say anything. Promise?' He sank with her on to the bowling green-smooth lawn, careless of his expensive suit, and she nodded silently as her eyes swept over his handsome face. 'I've been to see Sandra.'

'Blade!' She reared up like a scalded cat. 'You promised me you wouldn't, not yet, not till I could face it.'

'You didn't have to,' he said quietly as he pulled her back down beside him. 'I didn't plan to tell you anything about it. I just wanted to find out details, doctors, things like that so I could make my own enquiries. I didn't intend to leave a stone unturned——' He stopped abruptly. 'Hell, I'm not making a very good job of this. Amy...' He took her face in his hands as he gazed deep into her troubled eyes. 'You don't have the disease, you're safe, it's not going to happen.'

'What?' Time had stopped, suspended and hanging on a thread in the dusky stillness. 'Blade, what did you say?'

'You don't have it, Amy, I've checked, I'm sure.' He watched the colour flare and then recede in her face anxiously. 'I didn't mean to tell you like this, I was going to lead into it gradually to cut down the shock.' The buzzing in her ears was deafening but she fought against the faint feeling sweeping her body with

sickening weakness, and leant against him shakily.
This wasn't happening, it couldn't be, it was too much
like all the hopes and dreams she'd had in the last
few months to be true.

'Let me tell you now, from the beginning, and don't
say anything.' His arms were strong and secure as they
held her close and she nodded silently, her heart
pounding. She mustn't hope, not for a minute. It
would be a mistake. She knew it.

'I flew up to Scotland early this morning after ar-
ranging to meet Sandra's husband yesterday. She
wouldn't see me but, frankly, after what you'd told
me I didn't think I'd get too far with her anyway. I
met Jim for lunch in a hotel down the road from their
home; he's a good man.' She nodded again without
speaking. She vaguely remembered seeing him in the
background as she'd stumbled out of the house on
her last visit, but his face had been a blur through her
tears. 'Amy, how important is it to you that Sandra
is your sister?'

'What?' Her head jerked up as she stared into his
dark face. 'Oh, I don't know.' She shook her head
slowly. 'Not at all now really, too much has happened.'

'Well, she isn't related to you at all.' His arm tightened still further round her. 'And this next bit might
hurt a little. The couple you looked on as mother and
father weren't your parents.'

'Blade, I don't understand any of this.' She looked
at him, her eyes huge.

'Then let me explain. Apparently about three years
after Sandra was born her parents found out about
the disease when it began to show symptoms in the
mother. They had everything checked and the worst

was confirmed. They wanted more children but of course that was impossible, and so they concentrated on Sandra, spoiling her hopelessly and giving her everything she wanted. And then, when Sandra was seven, her mother's best friend got pregnant on a one-night stand while her husband was working away in the Far East or some such place. Apparently she couldn't face an abortion but neither could she keep the child, and so——' he turned and brought her face round to meet his fully '—they hatched a plan, an illegal plan.'

'Me?' she asked softly.

'You.' He nodded slowly. 'The four of them, Sandra included, went off for an extended holiday in Latin America and you were born there. Neither of the women had said to anyone they were pregnant, and when Sandra's mother claimed you were a surprise birth there was no reason for anyone to doubt it. Sandra's mother was thrilled with her new baby, the friend went back home and her husband never knew anything about it, everyone was happy—except Sandra.' He eyed her carefully. 'Apparently you were startlingly beautiful even then, and everything Sandra's mother had always wanted in a little girl. From what Jim told me, Sandra wasn't just pushed aside and neglected, they actually inflicted a mental cruelty of the worst kind. I should imagine along with the disease is a form of imbalance in the mind. Sandra has it and her mother certainly did.'

'Oh, Blade.' She shivered in the warm darkness. 'How terrible.'

'Yes.' His voice was grim now. 'Man's inhumanity to man. Jim knows her mind is sick, but he couldn't

believe what she'd said to you. Apparently she told
him you were upset at finding her so ill when he asked
why you left crying that time. She's eaten up with
hate, Amy, riddled with it, but he'll stay with her until
the end. He's that type of man.' He looked at her for
a long moment as she sat trying to absorb what he
had said. 'Would you like to see a picture of your
mother?'

'You have one?' Her face lit up as a sudden thought
occurred. 'Is she——'

'No, she's not alive Amy, I'm sorry.' He reached
into his pocket for a dogeared photograph. 'She died
shortly after she'd had you in some sort of accident,
which was one of the reasons Sandra's mother went
overboard. From that point she convinced herself she
really *had* given birth to you, you became hers.' He
placed the faded snapshot in her hand gently.

'It's me.' She looked down at the beautiful smiling
face as a little shiver snaked down her spine.

'Uncanny, isn't it?' Blade shook her gently as she
continued staring at the photograph in dumb shock.
'You understand what all this means, Amy? The
future is ours again to do with what we want. No
nightmares, no bad dreams. You can be yourself
again.'

'But I don't know who I am any more.' She raised
her head to stare into his dark eyes. 'It's a strange
feeling, Blade.'

'You're my wife.' He kissed her tenderly, the
burning passion that he was trying to keep in check
flaring through as he felt her response. 'And you'll
be our children's mother. But most of all you are what
you have become in the last twenty-two years. You

have an identity in your own right, sweetheart, compounded of all the things that have made you you. You are brave and strong and incredibly selfless, you're my beautiful, beautiful Amy and I love you more than life itself.'

She felt the tears hot on her face, but couldn't have explained why she was crying. Maybe it was for the parents who were never hers, the sister who had never been a sister, her mother who had been grateful to give her away, but then, through the tears, the glorious realisation burst like a ray of white-gold sunlight. She was crying also with relief, with thankfulness, and with deep, deep gratitude that she had come home at last. Blade was her family, he always had been from the moment they had met. In him she was complete.

'Let's go and make a baby, Blade.' She suddenly flung herself on him, smothering his face with kisses as she felt the hunger grow inside her. 'This is the first day of the rest of our life, and we are going to have fat bonny babies, hundreds of them. I want to make love all day long every day.' She began to laugh through the tears, her voice ecstatic. 'And all night too.'

'Sounds good to me.' His face was ablaze with relief at her reaction, his body hard and strong as he gathered her into him. 'But we're not going anywhere. This first one can be conceived under the stars with the heavens open above us.'

And he was.

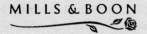

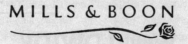

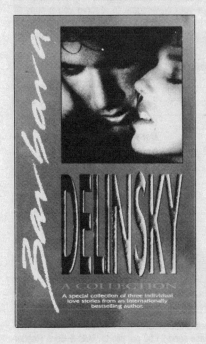

Next Month's Romances

Each month you can choose from a wide variety of romance with Mills & Boon. Below are the new titles to look out for next month, why not ask either Mills & Boon Reader Service or your Newsagent to reserve you a copy of the titles you want to buy – just tick the titles you would like and either post to Reader Service or take it to any Newsagent and ask them to order your books.

Please save me the following titles:	Please tick	✓
TRIAL BY MARRIAGE	*Lindsay Armstrong*	
ONE FATEFUL SUMMER	*Margaret Way*	
WAR OF LOVE	*Carole Mortimer*	
A SECRET INFATUATION	*Betty Neels*	
ANGELS DO HAVE WINGS	*Helen Brooks*	
MOONSHADOW MAN	*Jessica Hart*	
SWEET DESIRE	*Rosemary Badger*	
NO TIES	*Rosemary Gibson*	
A PHYSICAL AFFAIR	*Lynsey Stevens*	
TRIAL IN THE SUN	*Kay Thorpe*	
IT STARTED WITH A KISS	*Mary Lyons*	
A BURNING PASSION	*Cathy Williams*	
GAMES LOVERS PLAY	*Rosemary Carter*	
HOT NOVEMBER	*Ann Charlton*	
DANGEROUS DISCOVERY	*Laura Martin*	
THE UNEXPECTED LANDLORD	*Leigh Michaels*	

If you would like to order these books in addition to your regular subscription from Mills & Boon Reader Service please send £1.90 per title to: Mills & Boon Reader Service, Freepost, P.O. Box 236, Croydon, Surrey, CR9 9EL, quote your Subscriber No:.................................. (if applicable) and complete the name and address details below. Alternatively, these books are available from many local Newsagents including W H Smith, J Menzies, Martins and other paperback stockists from 13 January 1995.

Name:..

Address:..

...............................Post Code:........................

To Retailer: If you would like to stock M&B books please contact your regular book/magazine wholesaler for details.

You may be mailed with offers from other reputable companies as a result of this application. If you would rather not take advantage of these opportunities please tick box. ☐